RUMORS OF THE MARVELOUS

By the Author

NOVELS

MORNINGSTAR

BIG THUNDER

MOONTOWN

SHORT STORY COLLECTIONS

SPOOK CITY -WITH CLIVE BARKER AND RAMSEY CAMPBELL

RUMORS OF THE MARVELOUS

CEMETERY DANCE SELECT: PETER ATKINS

SCREENPLAYS

HELLBOUND: HELLRAISER II

HELLRAISER III: HELL ON EARTH

HELLRAISER: BLOODLINE

WISHMASTER

THE PALACE OF VARIETIES
——— PROUDLY PRESENTS ———

FROM DISTANT SHORES

RUMORS OF THE MARVELOUS

THRICE NIGHTLY
MATINEES SUNDAY

*Management bears no responsibilty
for mortification of the flesh*

GHOST STORIES
BY
PETER ATKINS

SHADOWRIDGE PRESS

RUMORS OF THE MARVELOUS
First U.S edition published March 2017
by Shadowridge Press

This work was previously published in the
United Kingdom as a limited edition
by The Alchemy Press, 2011

Book layout and design by Robert Barr
Cover concept by Peter Atkins

ISBN: 978-0-9897796-9-2

shadowridgepress.com

To my mother,

Gwen Atkins

And—because they refused
to wait their turn—to my nieces,

Gemma Hawksworth
and
Karyn Davis

Contents

INTRODUCTION

Marvelous, yes.

It might seem an odd claim to make about stories replete with melting men, ghost-girls with forked tongues, nasty green figurines and their even nastier protectors (or ... physical manifestations? Familiars?), vampire paintings, and cheerfully vengeful vigilantes armed with 'a pool cue, a pickle fork, and an active imagination'. But the secret's in the charm.

Peter Atkins' stories are indeed marvelous in the old, classical, *Oxford English Dictionary* sense: that is, 'causing of great wonder'. There are monsters here, alright. And some of them are going to eat you. But in Atkins-land, the three Weird Sisters—very weird indeed, and very deadly—have an even weirder father who, upon his death, leaves them a fragment of a song he didn't write, and 'the afternoon of September the seventh, Nineteen-sixty-three, as it appeared in New Brighton, England between the hours of two and five.' And you will find yourself sharing in the disquieting but unmistakable joy this bequeathal brings.

You'll never want to meet the aforementioned caretakers of those little green figurines. But you'll wish you had one.

You'll never want to visit what's left of the early '70s Liverpool Atkins evokes so vividly in 'The Mystery'. But you'll mourn its passing.

You might not wish to buy a book from the frumpy little beat girl in 'Frumpy Little Beat Girl'. But you'll hope—fervently—that she looks upon you 'not with contempt but with delight.'

Because like most of the significant artists who've contributed to the marvels of horror literature—King and Campbell, Machen and Blackwood, hell, Kipling and Stevenson—Peter Atkins is just plain good company. His Weird Sisters are named Chinchilla, Diamante, and Sam. His murderous revenants and fallen angels sing soulful (if not particularly reverent) gospel and leave frostbite kisses. His demons may well devour you, but they'll show you the night sky first.

In his 1898 introduction to the Scribner edition of Robert Louis Stevenson's *Valima Letters*, Sidney Colvin said that to meet the man was to be immediately overwhelmed by 'the charm of his talk, which was irresistibly sympathetic and inspiring, and no less full of matter than of mirth.' I hope you one day have the chance to sit down with Pete Atkins and talk *Doctor Who* or Roxy Music or Sax Rohmer or gas station sandwiches wrapped in plastic. But until then, these stories should provide at least a passable substitute for the pleasures of his company.

I didn't give Pete the nickname 'Nicest Guy in Horror'. But it's apt, both in describing the man and his work. There's so much light, laughter, surprise, and delight in this book. So many marvels, rumored and otherwise.

Of course, none of them will save you. But for a while—while you're reading—you might not mind so very much.

Glen Hirshberg
Claremont, California
May, 2011

RUMORS OF THE MARVELOUS

STACY AND HER IDIOT

- 1 -

You know, soon as the fat guy mentioned his contact in the 18th Street gang, I should've just walked away.

Wasn't that I gave a shit who he knew or didn't. It was the naked and stupid *pride* in his voice—you know, pulling that outlaw-by-association crap that only people who've spent their whole lives *without* association with outlaws can be bothered to pull. So he was bullshitting. BFD. Except that bullshitting is just a polite term for short-order lying, which meant that this fat sack of shit—who I'd known for all of three minutes—was already fucking lying to me.

Like I cared where he scored his drugs. Like it's my business. Here's how it should go. Money. Drugs. Thanks. Seeya. Have a nice life and try showing some mercy to the Cheeze-Whiz, you fat fuck. But no, he's got to start in with the anecdotes about his gangsta compadre. Which means I'm bored and annoyed so I do something stupid. I don't take a line. Don't even open the bag. I just want out of there as fast as possible. Real dumb. Felony level dumb. But I got two things in mitigation: I'd been clean and sober for ninety days so I didn't want to risk even a sample buzz; and I'd gotten this lardass's number from Paulie Benson and Paulie and me had never had a problem. So I cut Shamu off mid-story while he's gearing up to tell me just how many guys his guy has killed in the course of his illustrious career down there on 18th Street, throw him the money, take the packet and fuck off.

Takes me forty minutes to get back to Silverlake because some moron tries to make a left on Cahuenga at Franklin and gets side-swiped by the '92 Camaro that had the light. Jimmy Fitz and Stacy are spitting at each other in come-down by the time I let myself in and throw the packet at them. Stacy's right there with the mirror, the blade, and the straw—because, you know, nothing else really matters—but Jimmy looks at me hopefully.

"Change?" he says, like it's actually a possibility.

What fucking planet did Stacy find this guy on? I do him the kindness of not laughing out loud and head for my bedroom. Neither of them were going to be needing me for the next couple of hours.

Stacy was the sister of my best friend back in Jersey, so I was kind of obliged to like her, or at least to let her crash in my living room on this little California excursion of hers. But this Jimmy Fitz character was just some douchebag she'd let pick her up somewhere along the way and I didn't owe him jackshit. So you can imagine how happy I was when it was his voice that woke me less than half an hour later.

" 'the *fuck*?!" he was saying. " 'the *fuck*?!" And he kept saying it, little louder each time, until I finally got the message that it was for my benefit. It was the retard version of a gentle knock on the door and a polite 'terribly sorry to wake you, Ms. Donnelly, but there's something we need to talk about'.

I got up without bothering to throw any extra clothes on so I didn't realize I was treating J-Fitz to the classic halter-top and panties peepshow until he gave me that look. You know, *that* look. Seen it all my life from dipshits like him. Too bad you're a dyke, it says, because, man, is that an ass I'd like to tap. Prick. Stacy noticed it too and didn't seem to be much happier about it than I was, but she was much more concerned with the other little problem, the one that had gotten her boyfriend all worked up in the first place.

I'd already guessed the coke was fake—junkies rarely wake you up for any reason other than the absence of a fix—but it was a little odder than that. The package I'd brought was split open on the coffee table and the powder was scattered everywhere, which I'd normally have put down to the little tykes' adorable eagerness to get at the goodies. This time, though, it also allowed me an unobstructed view of the packet's surprise crackerjack gift.

It was a severed finger.

Guy's finger from the look of it – hair above the knuckle and shit – and it appeared to have been removed by a knife that could have been sharper and cleaner. It was still wearing a gold ring, which meant that whoever put the finger in the package meant for the ring to be part of the message. It was a signet ring, pearl inlay on black onyx, with a simple design – a central upright, like a capital 'I', with a curlicue at the top shooting off to the right and another at the bottom, shooting off to the left.

"I've seen that before," I said.

"The *finger*?" said Stacy.

"Don't be stupid," Jimmy Fitz said. "She means the ring."

"Oh," said Stacy, all offended. "Like the ring isn't on the fucking finger?"

"Yeah, but if the finger was on a fucking *hand*, and the hand was on a fucking *person*, then it's not quite the same as . . ."

"Shut up, both of you," I said. "I don't mean the finger or the ring. I mean what's on the ring."

"That sign thing?"

"The symbol, yeah."

"Where'd you see it?"

"It was on a wall."

"Like, painted?"

"Something like that," I said.

I'd figured it was gang graffiti. Not a tag I'd seen before but it's not like LA was, you know, running out of gangs any time soon. It was the same symbol as on the ring, though a little less well rendered. But then blood isn't as easy to paint with as you might think.

It was scrawled on the bare wall just above the head of the corpse, which was lying on the stripped bed in the second bedroom of some rented house in the Valley that one of Dominic Kinsella's crews was using for a porno shoot. Proponents of the good old American work-ethic will be glad to know that the shoot was continuing uninterrupted on the other side of the wall while the body turned blue. And the icing on the are-you-fuckin-kiddin-me cake was that the door to the room with the body wasn't even locked. I'd been delivering some high-end candy for cast and crew and had wandered in there by accident because I'd thought it was the door to the bathroom.

I had about five seconds to stare at the corpse—practically bisected by a close-range shotgun blast—before the Second Assistant Director followed me in there and closed the door carefully. He gave me an apologetic grimace, the semi-embarassed kind, the kind that's more suited to a Maitre D' telling you there's going to be a ten minute wait for your table, and raised his finger to his lips.

"The fuck is this?" I said, quietly enough.

"It was here when we came to set up," he said. "We're keeping the door closed so as not to upset the girls. Mister Kinsella's been informed."

Oh, well that was alright then. Long as Mister Kinsella had been informed. "What's *wrong* with you?" I asked, somewhat rhetorically.

"Look," he said. "It's nothing to do with us. It's going to be taken care of. Would you just *leave*, please? People are trying to work here."

So I left.

The hell else was I going to do? No rats in the Donnelly house.

But no fucking idiots either. I'd had a fine old time in the underworld but I was done. Done using. Done dealing. I mean, it wasn't like I was going to get, you know, a *job* or anything—it's not like there weren't plenty of other interesting ways for a girl to make an undeclared living, but from that point on I was staying in the shallow end. And I'd been there safe and happy, three months clean, until Stacy and her idiot showed up needing a favor and having no numbers of their own to call. And now this. Nice.

"What does it mean?" Stacy said.

"It's a rune," said James Fitzgerald, PhD.

"Whoa. Gold star, Frodo," I said. "Been getting down with your dad's copy of *Led Zeppelin IV* or something?"

"Fuck you," he said. Guess he was over his little crush on me.

"But what does it *mean*?" Stacy asked again. Jimmy shrugged, shook his head. They both looked at me.

I had no idea what the stupid *symbol* meant, but I could unfortunately make an educated guess as to what was going on. That fat motherfucker had been so busy jerking himself off with his second-hand thug-life stories that he'd given me a packet intended for someone else, someone for whom the fake drugs and the signet ring would be a very clear message.

"Reprisal killing," I said. "Gang war."

- 2 -

Now, how stupid would Jimmy Fitz and Stacy have to be to turn around the next morning and go back for their money?

Yeah. That stupid. Which is exactly how fucking stupid they were.

Crack of dawn they were gunning their car, full of caffeine and attitude, pumped and primed to head over to Hollywood and teach my new friend Orca that they're the sort of people around with whom one does not fuck.

I was still sleeping and knew nothing about it, of course, or I would've strapped them in the kiddie chairs and distracted them with cartoons and Vicodin. Figured they'd probably gone sight-seeing when I got up. The beach, maybe, or Grauman's Chinese. They wouldn't be the only strung-out white trash trying their Skechers out for size in John Wayne's footprints. The packet, the powder, and the unlucky bastard's finger were still on the coffee table. It wasn't until later that I remembered what *wasn't* still on the table—the post-it note with Roscoe Arbuckle's address on it—and that was long after I'd driven over to see Paulie Benson to try to get a handle on just what kind of trouble we might be in the middle of.

Paulie'd moved into a movie star's house for the summer. Least that's how he described it to people. I mean, nice house and all, but 'movie star' was probably stretching it. Longtime customer of Paulie's who was up in Toronto shooting a couple of straight-to-video action flicks back-to-back. It'd keep him busy eight or nine weeks and so Paulie got to play Lord of the Manor for a couple months in return for leaving a few Red Cross packages in strategic locations around the house for when not-even-Vin-Diesel got back.

It was still mid-morning, but Paulie's party never stops. Pretty boys and girls in and around the pool. Customers and colleagues drinking and snorting. I managed to get Paulie alone though and run things by him and the good news was he saw it my way. Figured me and the morons were just crossfire pedestrians who wouldn't be anybody's problem provided we played nice, gave the man his ball back, and kept our mouths shut. He calmed me down enough that I hung out a while, had a shot or two, and thought about flirting with any of the girls who looked like they might be interested in playing for my team. Some Spanish chick was telling me about her last incarnation when I suddenly remembered the missing post-it note and sobered up real fast.

I made it back from the Hills in a pretty impressive eighteen minutes and grabbed my phone. Jumbo picked up on the first ring.

"Harold," he said.

"That your *first* name?" I said. Because, you know, really.

"It is," he said. "Who wants to know?"

"Harold," I said, "we met yesterday. Helped each other out on that retail question?"

"Uh-huh," he said. Real non-committal real quick.

"There was an item, unsolicited and surplus to requirements, in the recent order. I'm an honest person, Harold, so I want you, and anybody else it may concern, to know that I'm going to return it. And that I'm very cognizant of what is, and what isn't, my business. Do we understand each other?"

"Uh-huh," he said again. Little friendlier this time.

"Would now be convenient, Harold?"

"Uh-huh," he said, and hung up.

He hadn't mentioned any other visitors he might have had that morning, and I'd figured that was best, too. For all I knew, they'd got lost or distracted and I could get it all dealt with before they fucked it up for everybody. Or they might be dead. Dominic Kinsella, or whoever it was that was pulling Harold's strings, might have already had people over at the fat bastard's place once he'd been apprised of yesterday's little mix-up.

I thought for a brief moment about getting hold of a gun. But here's what I know about guns: First; an exit wound is bigger than an entrance wound. Second; if you're checking out put it in your mouth not at your temple. Third; don't point it at someone unless you're damn sure you've got the balls to pull the trigger because, if you don't and they do, they'll take it off you and send you straight to that corner of Hell reserved for dumb fucks who shouldn't play with guns.

That's it. Double it and add tax and it's still sweet fuck-all. None of it *bad* information, but none of it front-end practical like, you know, loading, cocking, aiming, firing. So I was going to go on good faith, on the principle that if everybody kept their heads, we'd be fine. I blew the excess talc off the finger, put it in a baggie, shoved the baggie in my pocket, and headed over.

Harold disappointed me. I'd been polite and upfront with him and was walking into his place alone and unarmed to do the right thing. But Harold wasn't alone. There was another guy in there with him. Young, muscular, tousled hair all Brad Pitt blonde with dark roots. I could give a shit. His muscles looked like they'd been sculpted in a high-end gym rather than earned on the street, and he'd dressed himself in a camo jacket and steel-toed boots to look tough. Yeah. Real tough. Abercrombie & Fitch go Baghdad.

"Thought we were going to have a private chat," I said to Harold.

"Shut up, you dyke bitch," the kid said, which spoke well for his gaydar if not for his manners. I jabbed two stiff fingers into his Adam's apple without taking my eyes off Harold. Call me touchy. Girl's got feelings.

Harold was kind of cool. Didn't even look down as his Seacrest-on-steroids hit the floor gagging. Maybe this wasn't going to go as badly as I thought.

"Stay down, Matthew," Harold said, and treated me to the ghost of an admiring smile. "The lady apparently knows her business."

I reached for my pocket. Harold backed off a couple of feet. "I'm

STACY AND HER IDIOT

just here to return this," I said, my fingers closing around the baggie.

"Why don't you just hang onto it?" said Harold. He moved fast for a fat guy. The taser was in his hand before I even registered the odd and eager glint in his eye, and the stinger hit my chest before I could move. The voltage slammed through me, driving my body into a spastic dance, and I blacked out.

- 3 -

Don't know if you've ever gone any kind of distance bound and gagged in the trunk of an Oldsmobile, but I don't recommend it.

The ride was rough enough to begin with and the last twenty minutes—which, from the feel of it, was over the kind of ground yet to be reached by civilization—was actually painful. Still, I had lots to think about and it helped to distract me. Harold. Fucking Harold. Had to hand it to the fat prick, he was the motherfucking King of Misdirection. Not just small-scale—the asshole Malibu muscle to keep my attention off his boss getting the drop on me—but big-picture shit, too; all that crap about his 18th Street buddy the night before must've been just snow, a little blizzard of bullshit to encourage my contempt and stop me from reading Harold right while he handed me exactly the package he wanted me to have. Still didn't know *why*, of course, but I knew that Harold wasn't what I'd thought at all. Harold was a player. Problem was I had no idea what the game was.

The car stopped, and I heard the driver and passenger doors slam and footsteps come around to the back. The desert light was blinding after the darkness of the trunk and it took me a few seconds to bring Harold and Matthew into focus. They were both standing there and looking down at me. I've had better moments. Harold had a proprietary excitement in his eyes that I didn't like at all. Matthew was excited too, but in a more immediately understandable manner. He'd unzipped his pants and his cock was right out there in full view. He was stroking it. Not enough to get it leaking but enough to keep it interested while he pled his case.

"Just let me put it in," he was saying, trying hard to make it sound like a reasonable request. He was, by the way, talking to Harold not to me. "Just straight in and up. Just enough to let her know. Remind her who's in charge here."

Harold didn't answer him, though he did throw an apparently casual glance at his muscle's love-muscle that was enough to tell me more about Harold than I really needed to know.

Matthew grinned down at me. "Middle of the Mojave," he said. "Miles from anywhere. Go ahead and scream." He reached down and pulled the duct tape off my mouth. I neither screamed nor said a word, just kept my eyes fixed coldly on his.

"Think you're tough, don't you?" he said. "How about I shove this in your mouth?" He gave a demonstrative tug on his dick. I opened my mouth, wide, and then slammed my teeth together hard and fast in a little preview of what he could expect if he tried it. He flinched instinctively and raised his fist, ready to smash it into my face.

"No," said Harold. "We don't mark the meat." He turned and headed away from the car, speaking to Matthew over his shoulder. "Zip it up. Behave yourself. And bring her."

- 4 -

The only structure anywhere in sight was a shack, which I guess is where Harold had changed into his black robe, but the event was scheduled to take place behind it, out in the open, in a small and shallow basin-like depression in the sandy soil. That's where Matthew had brought me and where, after first pressing the taser hard against my throat to discourage any funny business, he'd surprisingly slashed the duct tape off my wrists and ankles with a serious looking knife and then, keeping the taser in plain sight, backed off to the perimeter of the basin, leaving me standing in the center.

Harold was on the perimeter, too, but he and Matthew were a good twenty feet apart, triangulating me.

"As you can see," Harold said, already sweating like the fat pig he was in his heavy black robe under the low desert sun, "the ground has been prepared."

Yeah, well that was one way of describing the various bloody pieces of Jimmy Fitz that decorated the four corners of the area as if marking the bases on a ballpark diamond in Hell. Poor Jimmy's idiot head stared at me from home plate, dead eyes still holding an echo of astonishment, jaw held open by a swizzle stick and the cave of its open mouth filled with small rose petals of a delicate and almost translucent yellow. The petals would have struck me as, you know, an unusual grace-note but forgive me if I was a little low on appreciation of aesthetic fucking incongruity right at that moment.

"Where's Stacy?" I asked.

Harold glanced at his watch. "Oh, I'm sure she's back with Paulie by now," he said, and smiled.

I didn't say anything, and I hope to Christ I didn't let him see anything, but he knew I was feeling it all right, and he took a moment or two to let it take a good firm hold.

"If it's any consolation," he said eventually, "you don't have long to worry about being played for such a fool. The sun is soon to dip below the earth and the betrayal of friends will be far from your mind."

I might have laughed at the strange formality that had crept into Harold's speech if I wasn't busy realizing that I might be quite seriously fucked here. I still didn't know exactly what Harold had in mind but I was pretty fucking sure I wasn't going to enjoy it. Still, Stacy and Paulie were on my list now. They'd served me to this insane bastard like a party favor and I found a little comfort, or at least distraction, in thinking about how slowly I was going to kill them if I managed to get out of here alive.

The back door of the shack opened and an old woman came out.

At first glance, she could have been some ancient relative of mine from the old country. Big black-Irish bitch turning brick-house solid in her final years. She walked, poorly, with the aid of a stick, the ornamental handle of which was the dry skull of a dead hawk. One of her eyes was sea-green. The other was dead. And the skin of her face was white. I don't mean pale. I mean *white*. White as the paper you're reading this on. White as the roof of the world.

She reached the perimeter and stopped, keeping the same kind of semi-formal distance from Harold and Matthew as they did from each other. Her head swiveled on her neck to face Harold with a leathery creaking so brittle-sounding that you'd swear there was nothing liquid inside her.

"I have come as contracted," she cawed at Harold, "to bear witness to the keeping of your covenant."

Harold inclined his elephantine head as elegantly as he could. "The offering has been brought," he said, "unmarked and unbound, and bearing the sigil."

Christ on crack, what was this? A fucking Masonic lodge? The desiccate old crone turned to look at me.

"Welcome, child," she said. "I am The Planet Trilethium."

Believe me, I'd love to have laughed. But her voice had no humor in it, nor any trace of self-consciousness. She was speaking her true name and, as she did, it seemed that her dead eye glistened for a second as if there were a light far behind its surface, as if it was watching from a very long way away.

And I swear to God the sand beneath my feet shifted in response.

And sighed.

I felt it all almost drain out of me then, felt the way you have to figure the prey feels when the predator's jaw closes on it. You've seen it, right? In those nature films? They just go limp at the last, accepting it, letting it happen. There's probably a comfort there.

But, as my sainted mother used to say, Fuck That Shit.

Considering Matthew was the only one with actual weapons in his hand – the taser and the knife – I must have looked like a moron running at him instead of one of the others. But I figured him as the nearest to an amateur and, besides, what the fuck did I have to lose? I belted toward him, fast, straight, and furious. And sure enough, the dickwad instinctively fired the taser immediately instead of waiting for me to get close enough. I hardly even had to sidestep. The look on his face when the stinger went wide was so fucking sweet that I almost paused to savor it. But I didn't. Because that would have meant less momentum when I drove my boot into the kneecap of the leg he was putting his weight on. He screamed like a girl and, starting to go down, swung wildly with his knife, which was just what I wanted. I got a clean grip, snapped his wrist in two, grabbed the knife from his useless fingers and took a whole luxurious second to let him have a good look at it and see what was coming.

I didn't get a clean swipe at the fucker's eyes, because Harold's three hundred pounds suddenly slammed into me from behind, but even so the blade ended up hilt-deep through Matthew's upper cheek and it must have been angled upward enough to sever something important in what passed for his brain because he suddenly stopped moving altogether.

Harold grabbed at me before I could either steady myself or get the knife back and I only managed a half turn before he had me in a bear hug. We did some half-hearted wrestling, my forearms flapping around pretty uselessly, grabbing at his robe and his jacket beneath, and I tried to get my knee up to find wherever his minuscule balls hid beneath his mountainous gut, but it was no use. After a few seconds of letting me struggle, he slammed the flat of his arm against the side of my head and I went limp long enough to let him carry me back to the center of the basin and drop me there, still semi-dazed.

Harold was back at the perimeter before I could get to my feet. I saw him give an apologetic look to The Planet Trilethium, but she seemed, if anything, mildly amused.

Despite my ringing head, my blood was up now and I'd have been perfectly happy to take another run at the fat sack of shit, maybe try and sink my teeth into the meat of his throat and rip his fucking windpipe out, but the desert had other ideas.

The sand was rippling.

Slowly. Not like an earthquake. Like an ocean. Like an ocean with its depths disturbed, as if something far below was waking and moving and would soon break surface.

The Planet Trilethium sighed in anticipation, the breath rattling in her ancient open mouth like a reptile hiss.

Behind me, the sun was flattening as it reached the horizon.

"You have come to the appointed place," Harold called out. "You have come to the appointed hour."

It was actually hard to keep my footing now, the desert beneath me bucking and dipping and the speed of its impossible movements increasing. Harold had one last thing to say.

"And you bear the sign of the appointed one."

I planted my feet apart enough to let me keep my balance and stay upright as I found his eyes in the vanishing light and locked on them.

"Check your pocket, bitch," I said.

What, you think I wrestled the fat fuck to cop a feel?

Harold's hand flew beneath his robe to ferret in the pocket of his jacket and I could tell the precise moment that his hand closed around the baggie with the severed finger by the way his face crumpled past anger and disbelief into something much more satisfying.

I began running out of the center of the basin, hurdling the raging earth, and Harold—screaming like a baby, I'm delighted to say—ran to intercept me, holding the baggie out like he was going to force the ring on me again. But the Sun was gone. And rules is rules, right? Appointed hour, and all that shit.

The Planet Trilethium opened her mouth. Real wide. And a tongue the color of bruises and the length of a garden hose flew at Harold, wrapped around his throat, lifted his massive bulk effortlessly, and slammed him, back first, onto the bucking desert floor in the center of the basin.

I'm a girl who watches her manners, so I'd like to have stopped to thank her but, you know. Busy running. And I really don't think she did it for me anyway. I was utterly irrelevant now, thank fuck, both to her and to whatever was rising from beneath the desert floor. They didn't need me. They had Harold.

I didn't stop running till I reached the Olds on the far side of the shack. I didn't look back even then. You couldn't have paid me to look back. Because, God knows, the sounds were bad enough.

I was ready to hotwire the car if I needed to—because, you know, I've got mad skills—but the key was right there in the ignition. I had no idea which way the freeway was but as long as The Planet Trilethium was behind me then I was going in the right direction.

I drove for a long time. Let midnight come and go. It was after I'd stopped for a burger somewhere off the I-10 that I discovered there was a cell-phone in the glove compartment.

I seriously thought about giving Paulie a call.

But, you know, why spoil the surprise?

BETWEEN THE COLD MOON AND THE EARTH

They only brushed his cheek for a second or two, but her lips were fucking *freezing*.

"Christ, Carol," he said. "Do you want my coat?"

She laughed. "What for?" she asked.

"Because it's one in the morning," he said. "And you're cold."

"It's summer," she pointed out, which was undeniably true but wasn't really the issue. "Are you going to walk me home, then?"

Michael had left the others about forty minutes earlier. Kirk had apparently copped off with the girl from Woolworth's that they'd met inside the pub so Michael and Terry had tactfully peeled away before the bus-stop and started walking the long way home around Sefton Park. He could've split a taxi-fare with Terry but, given that they were still in the middle of their ongoing argument about the relative merits of T.Rex and Pink Floyd and that it was still a good six months before they'd find Roxy Music to agree on, they'd parted by unspoken consent and Michael had opted to cut across the park alone.

Carol had been standing on the path beside the huge park's large boating lake. He'd shit himself for a moment when he first saw the shadowed figure there, assuming the worst—a midnight skinhead parked on watch ready to whistle his mates out of hiding to give this handy glam-rock faggot a good kicking—but Carol had been doing nothing more threatening than staring out at the center of the lake and the motionless full moon reflected there.

"Alright, Michael," she'd said, before he'd quite recognized her in the moonlight, and had kissed his cheek lightly in further greeting before he'd spoken her name. Now, he fell into step beside her and they began to walk the long slow curve around the lake.

"God, Carol. Where've you been?" he asked. "Nobody's seen you for months."

It was true. Her mum had re-married just before last Christmas and they'd moved. Not far away, still in the same city, but far enough for sixteen-year-olds to lose touch.

"I went to America," Carol said.

Michael turned his head to see if she was kidding. "You went to *America*?" he said. "What d'you mean, you went to America? When? Who with?"

Her eyes narrowed for a moment as if she were re-checking her facts or her memory. "I think it was America," she said.

"You *think* it was America?"

"It might have been an imaginary America," she said, her voice a little impatient. "Do you want to hear the fucking story or not?"

Oh. Michael didn't smile nor attempt to kiss her, but he felt like doing both. Telling stories—real, imagined, or some happy collision of the two—had been one of the bonds between them, one of the things he'd loved about her. Not the only thing of course. It's not like he hadn't shared Kirk and Terry's enthusiastic affection for her astonishingly perfect breasts and for the teasingly challenging way she had about her that managed to suggest two things simultaneously: That, were circumstances to somehow become magically right, she might .. you know .. actually *do it* with you; and that you were probably and permanently incapable of ever conjuring such circumstance. But her stories, and her delight in telling them, were what he'd loved most and what, he now realized, he'd most missed. So yes, he said, he wanted to hear the story.

There was some quick confusion about whether she'd got there by plane or by ship—Carol had never been a big fan of preamble—but apparently what mattered was that, after a few days, she found herself in a roadside diner with a bunch of people she hardly knew.

They were on a road-trip and had stopped for lunch in this back-of-beyond and unpretentious Diner—a place which, while perfectly clean and respectable, looked like it hadn't been painted or refurbished since about 1952. They were in a booth, eating pie and drinking coffee. Her companions were about her age—but could, you know, *drive* and everything. Turned out boys in America could be just as fucking rude as in Liverpool. One of them—Tommy, she thought his name was – was giving shit to the waitress. Hoisting his empty coffee mug, he was leaning out of the booth and looking pointedly down the length of the room.

"Yo! Still need a refill here!" he shouted to the counter.

Carol stood up and, announcing she was going to the ladies' room, slid her way out of the booth. Halfway down the room, she crossed paths with the waitress, who was hurrying toward their booth with a coffee-pot. The woman's name-tag said *Cindi*, a spelling Carol had never seen before and hoped could possibly be short for Cinderella because that'd be, you know, great. Carol spoke softly to her, nodding back towards Tommy, who was impatiently shaking his empty coffee mug in the air.

"Don't mind him, love," Carol said. "He's a bit of a prick, but I'll make sure he leaves a nice tip."

Cindi, who looked to be at least thirty and harried-looking, gave her a quick smile of gratitude. "Little girls' room's out back, sweetheart," she said.

Carol exited the main building of the diner and saw that a separate structure, little more than a shack really, housed the bathrooms. She started across the graveled parking-lot, surrounded by scrub-grass that was discolored and overgrown, looking down the all-but-deserted country road—the type of road, she'd been informed by her new friends, which was known as a two-lane blacktop. The diner and its shithouse annex were the only buildings for as far as her eye could see, apart from a hulking grain silo a hundred yards or so down the road. As Carol looked in that desolate direction, a cloud drifted over the sun, dimming the summer daylight and shifting the atmosphere into a kind of prestorm dreariness. Carol shivered and wondered, not without a certain pleasure in the mystery, just where the hell she was.

Done peeing and alone in the bathroom, Carol washed her hands and splashed her face at the pretty crappy single sink that was all the place had to offer. The sound of the ancient cistern laboriously and noisily re-filling after her flush played in the background. Carol turned off the tap and looked for a moment at her reflection in the pitted and stained mirror above the sink. As the cistern finally creaked and whistled to a halt, the mirror suddenly cracked noisily across its width as if it was just too tired to keep trying.

"Fuckin' 'ell!" said Carol, because it had made her jump and because she didn't like the newly mis-matched halves of her reflected face. She turned around, ready to walk out of the bathroom, and discovered she was no longer alone.

A little girl—what, six, seven years old? —was standing, silent and perfectly still, outside one of the stall doors, looking up at her. Oddly, the little girl was holding the palm of one hand over her right eye.

"Oh shit," said Carol, remembering that she'd just said fucking hell in front of a kid. "I didn't know you were .." She paused, smiled, started over. "Hello, pet. D'you live around here?"

The little girl just kept looking at her.

"What's your name?" Carol asked her, still smiling but still getting no response. Registering the hand-over-the-eye thing, she tried a new tack. "Oh," she said. "Are we playing a game and nobody told me the rules? Alright then, here we go."

Raising her hand, Carol covered her own right eye with her palm. The little girl remained still and silent. Carol lowered her hand from her face. "Peek-a-boo," she said.

Finally, the little girl smiled shyly and lowered her own hand. She had no right eye at all, just a smooth indented bank of flesh.

Carol was really good. She hardly jumped at all and her gasp was as short-lived as could reasonably be expected.

The little girl's voice was very matter-of-fact. "Momma lost my eye-patch," she said.

"Oh. That's a shame," said Carol, trying to keep her own voice as equally everyday.

"She's gonna get me another one. When she goes to town."

"Oh, well, that's good. Will she get a nice color? Do you have a favorite color?"

The little girl shrugged. "What are you, retarded?" she said. "It's an eye-patch. Who cares what color it is?"

Carol didn't know whether to laugh or slap her.

"You can go now, if you like," said the little girl. "I have to make water."

"Oh. Alright. Sure. Well, look after yourself," Carol said and, raising her hand in a slightly awkward wave of farewell, headed for the exit door. The little girl called after her.

"You take care in those woods now, Carol", she said.

"I hadn't told her my name," said Carol.

"Well, that was weird," Michael said.

Carol smiled, pleased. "*That* wasn't weird," she said. "It *got* weird. Later. After I got lost in the woods."

"You got lost in the woods?"

Carol nodded.

"Why'd they let you go wandering off on your own?"

"Who?"

"Your new American friends. The people you were in the café with."

"Ha. Café. *Diner*, stupid. We were in America."

"Whatever. How could they let you get lost?"

"Oh, yeah." She thought for a second, looking out to their side at the boating lake and its ghost moon. "Well, p'raps they weren't there to begin with. Doesn't matter. Listen."

Turned out Carol *did* get lost in the woods. Quite deep in the woods, actually. Heart of the forest, Hansel and Gretel shit, where the sunlight, through the thickening trees, was dappled and spotty and where the reassuring blue sky of what was left of the afternoon could be glimpsed only occasionally through the increasingly oppressive canopy of high leafy branches.

Carol was tramping her way among the trees and the undergrowth on the mossy and leaf strewn ground when she heard the sound for the first time. Faint and plaintive and too distant to be truly identifiable, it was nevertheless suggestive of something, something that Carol couldn't quite put her finger on yet. Only when it came again, a few moments later, did she place it. It was the sound of a lonely ship's horn in a midnight ocean, melancholy and eerie. Not quite as eerie, though, as the fact that once the horn had sounded this second time, all the other sounds stopped, all the other sounds that Carol hadn't even been consciously aware of until they disappeared; birdsong, the footsteps of unseen animals moving through the woods, the sigh of the breeze as it whistled through the branches.

The only sounds now were those she made herself; the rustle and sway of the living branches she was pushing her way through and the crackle and snap of the dead ones she was breaking beneath her. Carol began to wonder if moving on in the same direction she'd been going was that great of an idea. She turned around and started heading back and, within a few yards, stepping out from between two particularly close trees, she found herself in a small grove-like clearing that she didn't remember passing through earlier.

There was a downed and decaying tree-trunk lying in the leafy undergrowth that momentarily and ridiculously put Carol in mind of a park bench. But she really wasn't in the mood to sit and relax and it wasn't like there was, you know, a boating lake to look at the moon in or anything. So she kept moving, across the clearing, past the downed trunk, and stopped only when the voice spoke from behind her.

"What's your rush, sweetheart?"

Carol turned back. Sitting perched on the bench-like trunk was a sailor. He was dressed in a square-neck deck-shirt and bell-bottomed pants and Carol might have taken a moment to wonder if sailors still dressed like that these days if she hadn't been too busy being surprised just to see him at all. He was sitting in profile to her, one leg on the ground, the other arched up on the trunk and he didn't turn to face her fully, perhaps because he was concentrating on rolling a cigarette.

"Ready-mades are easier," the sailor said. "But I like the ritual - opening the paper, laying in the tobacco, rolling it up. Know what I mean?"

"I don't smoke," said Carol, which wasn't strictly true, but who the fuck was he to deserve the truth.

"You chew?" he asked.

"Chew what?"

"Tobacco"

"Eugh. No."

The sailor chanted something rhythmic in response, like he was singing her a song but knew his limitations when it came to carrying a tune:

"Down in Nagasaki,
Where the fellas chew tobaccy
And the women wicky-wacky-woo."

Carol stared at him. Confused. Not necessarily nervous. Not yet. She gestured out at the woods. "Where'd you come from?" she said.

"Dahlonega, Georgia. Little town North-east of Atlanta. Foot of the Appalachians."

That wasn't what she'd meant and she started to tell him so, but he interrupted.

"Ever been to Nagasaki, honeybun?"

"No."

"How about Shanghai?"

The Sailor was still sitting in profile to her. Talking to her, but staring straight ahead into the woods and beyond. He didn't wait for a reply. "Docked there once," he said. "Didn't get shore-leave. Fellas who did told me I missed something, boy. Said there were whores there could practically tie themselves in knots. Real limber. Mmm. A man likes that. Likes 'em limber."

Carol was very careful not to say anything at all. Not to move. Not to breathe.

"Clean, too," said the sailor. "That's important to me. Well, who knows? Maybe I'll get back there one of these days. Course, once they get a good look at me, I might have to pay extra." He turned finally to face her. "Whaddaya think?"

Half of his face was bone-pale and bloated, as if it had drowned years ago and been underwater ever since. His hair hung dank like seaweed and something pearl-like glinted in the moist dripping blackness of what used to be an eye-socket.

"Jesus Christ!" Carol said, frozen in shock, watching helplessly as the sailor put his cigarette in his half-ruined mouth, lit it, and inhaled.

"Calling on the Lord for salvation," he said. "Good for you. Might help." Smoke oozed out from the pulpy white flesh that barely clung to the bone beneath his dead face. "Might not."

He rose to his feet and grinned at her. "Useta chase pigs through the Georgia pines, sweet thing," he said, flinging his cigarette aside. "Let's see if you're faster than them little squealers."

And then he came for her.

❀

"I was a lot faster, though," said Carol. "But it still took me ten minutes to lose him."

"Fuck, Carol," said Michael. "That wasn't funny."

"I didn't say it was funny. I said it was weird. Remember?"

Michael turned to look at her and she tilted her face to look up at his, dark eyes glinting, adorably proud of herself. They'd walked nearly a full circuit of the lake now, neither of them even thinking to branch off in the direction of the park's northern gate and the way home.

"Well, it was weird alright," Michael said. "Creepy ghost sailor. Pretty good."

"Yeah," she said. "Turns out there was a ship went down there in the second world war. All hands lost."

"Went down in the woods. That was a good trick."

"It wasn't the *woods*. Didn't I tell you that? It was the beach. That's where it all happened."

"Was it Redondo?"

"The fuck's *Redondo*?" she said, genuinely puzzled.

"It's a beach. In America. I've heard of it. It's on that Patti Smith album."

"Oh, yeah. No. This wasn't in America. It was in Cornwall." She thought about it for a moment. "Yeah. Had to be Cornwall because of the rock pool."

"You didn't say anything about a rock pool."

"I haven't *told* you yet," she said, exasperated. "God, you're rubbish."

Michael laughed, even though something else had just hit him. He was walking on a moonlit night alone with a beautiful girl and it apparently wasn't occurring to him to try anything. He hadn't even put his arm around her, for Christ's sake. Terry and Kirk would give him such shit for this when he told them. He wondered for the first time if that was something Carol knew, if that was what had always been behind her stories, why she found them, why she told them, like some instinctive Scheherazade keeping would-be lovers at bay with narrative strategies. He felt something forming in him, a kind of sadness that he couldn't name and didn't understand.

"Is everything alright, Carol?" he asked, though he couldn't say why.

"Well, it is *now*," she said, deaf to the half-born subtext in his question. "I got away. I escaped. But that spoils the story, dickhead. You've got to hear what *happened* first."

The park was silver-gray in the light from the moon. He wondered what time it was. "The rock pool," he said.

"Exactly," she said, pleased that he was paying attention.

She hadn't seen it at first. Had kept moving along the deserted beach until the sandy shore gave way to rocky cave-strewn outcrops from the cliffs above the coastline. It was only when she clambered over an algae and seaweed coated rock wall that she found it. Orphaned from the sea and held within a natural basin formation, the pool was placid and still and ringed by several large boulders about its rim. It was about twenty feet across and looked to be fairly deep.

On one of the boulders, laid out as if waiting for their owner, were some items of clothing. A dress, a pair of stockings, some underwear. Carol looked from them out to the cool inviting water of the pool. A head broke surface as she looked, and a woman started swimming toward the rock where her clothes were. Catching sight of Carol, she stopped and trod water, looking at her suspiciously. "What are you doing?" she said. "Are you spying?" She was older than Carol, about her mum's age maybe, a good-looking thirty-five.

"No, I'm not," Carol said. "Why would I be spying?"

"You might be one of them," the woman said.

"One of who?"

The woman narrowed her eyes and looked at Carol appraisingly. "You know who," she said.

"No, I don't," Carol said. "And I'm not one of anybody. I was with some friends. We went to France. Just got back. The boat's down there on the beach."

"They've all got stories," the woman said. "That's how they get you."

"Who?! Stop talking shit, willya? I .." Carol bit her tongue.

For the first time, the woman smiled. "Are you moderating your language for me?" she said. "That's adorable."

Carol felt strangely flustered. Was this woman *flirting* with her?

"I understand," the woman said, still smiling, still staring straight into Carol's eyes. "I'm an older lady and you want to be polite. But, you know, I'm not really *that* much older." She stepped out of the pool and stood there right in front of Carol, glistening wet and naked. "See what I mean?" she said.

Carol felt funny. She swallowed. The woman kept her eyes fixed on Carol as she stepped very close to her. "I'm going to tell you a secret," she said, and leaned forward to whisper the secret in Carol's ear. "I'm real limber for my age."

Carol jumped back as the woman's voice began a familiar rhythmic chant.

"*Down in Nagasaki,*
Where the fellas chew tobaccy,
And the women wicky-wacky-woo."

Carol tried to run but the woman had already grabbed her by the throat. "What's your rush, sweetheart?" she said, and her voice was different now, guttural and amused. "Party's just getting started."

Carol was struggling in the choking grip. She tried to swing a fist at the woman's head but her punch was effortlessly blocked by the woman's other arm.

"Your eyes are so pretty," the woman said. "I'm going to have them for earrings."

Her mouth opened inhumanly wide. Her tongue flicked out with reptile speed. It was long and black and forked.

"But like I said," said Carol, "I escaped."

"How?" said Michael, expecting another previously unmentioned element to be brought into play, like a knife or a gun or a really sharp stick or a last-minute rescue from her Francophile friends from the recently-invented boat. But Carol had a different ending in mind.

"I walked into the Moon," she said.

Michael looked up to the night sky.

"No," said Carol. "Not that Moon. This one."

She was pointing out towards the center of the utterly calm lake and the perfect Moon reflected there. Looking at it with her, neither of them walking now, Michael felt the cold of the night as if for the first time. He waited in silence, afraid to speak, afraid to give voice to his questions, afraid that they would be answered.

She told another story then, the last, he knew, that his sweet lost friend would ever tell him, the tale of how the other Moon had many ways into and out of this world: Through placid lakes on summer evenings; through city streets on rain-slicked nights; from out the ocean depths for the eyes of lonely night-watch sailors.

And when she was done, when Michael could no longer pretend not to know in whose company he truly was, she turned to him and smiled a heartbreaking smile of farewell.

She looked beautiful in monochrome, in the subtle tones of the Moon that had claimed her for its own. Not drained of color, but richly re-imagined, painted in shades of silver, gray, and black, and delicate lunar blue. She looked almost liquid, as if, were Michael to reach out a hand and even try to touch her, she might ripple into strange expansions of herself.

"Thanks, Michael," she said. "I can make it home from here."

Michael didn't say anything. Didn't know what he could possibly find to say that the tears in his young eyes weren't already saying. The beautiful dead girl pointed a silver finger beyond him, in the direction of his life. "Go on," she said kindly. "Don't look back."

And he didn't look back, not even when he heard the impossible footsteps on the water, not even when he heard the shadow moon sigh in welcome, and the quiet lapping of the lake water as if something had slipped effortlessly beneath it.

He'd later hear the alternative versions of course – the stories of how, one moonlit night, Carol had walked out of the third-floor window of her step-father's house and the vile rumors as to why—but he would prefer, for all his days, to believe the story that the lost girl herself had chosen to tell him.

He continued home through the park, not even breaking step as his fingers sought and found the numb spot on his cheek, the frozen place where her cold lips had blessed him, waiting for her frostbite kiss to bloom in tomorrow's mirror.

KING OF
OUTER SPACE

- 1 -

She'd been crying herself to sleep for nearly a year now but it still didn't feel like a habit. It still felt new and raw.

Here's how it went: She'd do the bathroom stuff, get into bed, read for a while, remote some late-night host into TV life, kill the light, and close her eyes. And somewhere between the last sentences from the talk show and the first whispers from the dream country she'd be jerked awake by a body-racking sob and find her eyes were full of tears.

Her name was Marion Marshall, she was twenty-eight years old, and her fiancé was dead.

- 2 -

FADE IN

EXT. DEEP SPACE

Against a field of stars, a ROCKETSHIP hurtles

through the void. Flames shimmer from its
boosters, their majestic roar telling the
laws of physics to go fuck themselves.

The ship is a retro-futurist dream. Fins,
chrome, and streamlined splendor. Like the
child of some 1958 jam session between Werner
Von Braun and a hotshot from the design team
at Cadillac.

No. Screw that. You know what it's like? It's
like the Legion Of Super-Heroes clubhouse
from a 1963 issue of *Adventure Comics*. Turned
on its ass, fitted with a nose-cone and a
bunch of thrusters, and sent blasting
through the inter-galactic ether as if
Imagination had grabbed Science in the
schoolyard and slapped the little geek around
some till it knew its place.

DISSOLVE TO

INT. ROCKETSHIP COCKPIT

A big curved window offers an unobstructed
view of the cosmos and the walls are studded
with pieces of equipment picked up from a
yard-sale thrown by the guys who designed
The Quatermass Experiment.

Sitting in the single chair is JONATHAN KING,
astronaut. Mid-30s. Ruggedly handsome.
Spacesuit from the racks of the tailor who
dressed Adam Strange and Steve Zodiac. Skin-
tight and colorful. Heroic and decorative.
Stopping just short of the point at which

you'd question the wearer's sexual
preference.

CLOSE on King's eyes. Fixed on the window.
Flicking steadily from side to side,
systematically scanning the galactic vistas
through which he rides.

CLOSE on King's left hand. The fingers are
wrapped in sensor-tape, fiber-optic cables
trailing from them into a computer-input in
the chair's armrest. Pulses of light throb
down the cables.

CLOSE on the ship's monitor-screens - across
which streams of data play as the information
from his scanning eyes is electronically
stored.

WIDE - as King unhooks the sensors from his
fingers and walks over to the radio. He grabs
the handset - which looks suspiciously like
the bulky RCA mike Elvis used on Ed Sullivan
- and talks into it.

                    KING
        Hello? Hello? Can you hear me? Can ..

        CUT TO

                    - 3 -

Marion wasn't sure what woke her up. Groggy and confused, she
rolled over to blink her bedside clock's LCD into focus.
4:02 am.
After four. The little girl in her was relieved. She hated waking at

night to get up and pee or whatever because she was never quite sure that something supernatural wasn't waiting for her in the dark. But some long-forgotten Counsellor at some long-forgotten Summer Camp had once told her that it was only the four hours after midnight that were the dangerous ones and she'd lived by that wisdom ever since.

She was about to push the covers aside, ready to head to the bathroom, when she realized that it wasn't her bladder that had pulled her from sleep after all. It was a noise; low and barely-heard, a continuous stream of crackle and hiss like an AM station failing in a desert midnight. Marion padded her hand in a blind arc across her quilt and found the remote. She'd already hit the power button before registering that the TV hadn't been on until she'd done so. She killed it again before the infomercial had a chance to pitch itself into the darkness of her room and propped herself up on one elbow to try and locate the source of the sound.

It was coming from the drawer of her bedside table. Her hand was braver than her heart, reaching instinctively to pull the drawer open before she stopped it, suddenly convinced that she was misreading the sound. She heard it transform in her imagination, moving from the electronic to the animal, becoming chitinous and agitated, the sound of some multi-limbed insect monstrosity, a huge water-bug trapped and furious and eager to be free. A panic revulsion swept through her and, clicking on the reading lamp, she swung her legs around to sit on the edge of the bed, staring helplessly at the drawer.

Then she got it. Maybe it was the light, maybe it was taking a breath, maybe it was just the resurgent reason that came with a fuller wakefulness, but she suddenly knew precisely what the noise was. With a self-deprecating groan she pulled the drawer open.

Her Earthquake-Preparedness Kit wasn't much by Los Angeles standards and its components were all but hidden by the various un-filed receipts and other detritus of daily life that Marion regularly threw in the drawer to keep her surfaces tidy but some quick scrabbling revealed the flashlight, the first-aid box, and—finally—the tiny transistor radio.

She pulled it from the drawer, wondering how it had somehow turned itself on, and listened to the strange atonal music of its station-less signal as it seemed to strain for clarity and connection. An unbidden image came to her, straight from the World War II movies her father had loved and had tried in vain to make her love also; a soldier, lost behind enemy lines, trying desperately to find a frequency that would bring him nearer to home.

Her eyes had just registered the curious fact that the radio's power switch was firmly in the off position when the signal suddenly locked in. A voice, tiny and distant, emerged through the whistle and whine.

" .. you hear me? Marion? Marion, it's me. It's Jonathan."

She dropped it like she'd been bitten, her hand flying to her gasping mouth and tears filling her eyes as the old wounds opened again.

- 4 -

"And the radio shut off when you dropped it?"

"As soon as it hit the floor."

"Or as soon as you allowed the grief to flower properly?"

The therapist allowed herself a small smile. Gentle. Not smug at all. But Marion didn't like it anyway.

"My grief has no problem flowering. I water it every night," she said, and instantly regretted it. Juliana was particularly fond of extended metaphor and could often take these weekly sessions into such convolutions of figurative overlay that Marion sometimes wondered whether her eighty dollars were being spent on therapy or on an unacknowledged prep-course for some bad creative-writing class. She jumped back in before the other woman could run with it.

"But that's not the point," she said. "Yes, his voice went away. But I heard it."

"It was four in the morning," Juliana said. "You'd just woken up."

"I wasn't dreaming."

"No. I'm not suggesting you were." Juliana's eloquent hands moved in a symmetrical semaphore, placatory and soothing. "And I don't doubt that white noise from the radio is what woke you up. But .."

Marion interrupted. "What then?" she said. "I was still in a hypnagogic state and the voice was in my head?"

"Do you think?" Juliana said, crossing her perfect legs and cocking her head as if the thought had never occurred to her.

- 5 -

I resent her, Marion thought as she made the left onto Olive too sharply, the Chevy's ten-year-old engine giving a rattle of complaint.

I resent her trim little figure and her soft little voice. I resent her precise little hands and the way they weave their subtitles for the emotionally hard-of-hearing. I resent her black stockings and her high-heels. I bet all her male clients want to fuck her and I resent that too. I—

"Shit," Marion said out loud, glancing into her rear-view. She'd been so busy bitching that she'd missed the right on Buena Vista. Now she was screwed. Burbank always confused her and she knew there wasn't another road that would deposit her on the freeway for a couple of miles. She wondered if one of these side roads would at least take her down as far as Riverside. She could take that through the park and come out on Los Feliz.

Staring out the right to try and judge the streets, she found herself looking at a store window. The sadness overwhelmed her before she realized why it was. *House Of Secrets*, the sign said. She knew it well and had been there many times. Not recently though—no reason to, not now—and she hadn't realized it was this close to Juliana's office. It had always been Jonathan who drove when they made those Saturday morning trips to let him browse excitedly through the old comic-books in which the store specialized while she hovered near a rackful of action-figures trying to pretend she had the slightest interest in being there.

For a crazy moment, she considered parking the car and going in. Thought about peeling open one of those stupid plastic bags that the geeks cherished (*Museum-quality! Acid-free!*) and breathing in the mustiness of an old issue of *Mystery in Space* the way he'd used to do. And then she thought about the fresh bullets of pain that such a sensory trigger would fire into her and she jumped the light, ignoring the honking horn of the Accord she'd cut off, and headed south.

On Riverside, she switched from NPR to an oldies station and was rewarded with The Penguins singing "Earth Angel". The record was older than she was—her parents had still been in junior high when it was made—but she loved it. She knew enough about music to understand that its chord sequence was banal and its melody simplistic, but she knew enough about magic to understand that none of that mattered. Her mouth creased into something that felt unfamiliar and a little forced but was still undeniably a smile. She began to hum along as the road took her through Griffith Park.

By the time the Chevy was climbing the elevation that let the road look down on the concrete slash that called itself the Los Angeles River, The Penguins had been replaced by The Stones and their white-boy wannabe swagger. How come Eminem's a wigger, Marion thought, and Mick Jagger isn't? The static that was starting to break up Mick's little fantasy about a New York divorcee she put down to the altitude and then realized it wasn't meant to work that way. Puzzled, she looked down at the dial as if it were going to explain itself to her. Her finger was reaching out, ready to punch in another station, when the static overwhelmed the song completely. Its cacophony crescendoed and then cut off. There was a beat of utter silence—Marion heard a dog barking distantly somewhere in the park—and then a voice, a little out of phase in each of the car's four speakers:

"Marion, are you receiving me? Over."

- 6 -

Once upon a time, there was a little boy who lived in the forest. A kindly old woodsman had taken a shine to the boy, who looked to him often for answers to the questions that his wicked stepmother was too busy to consider.

"I was at the stream this morning," the boy said one day while the woodsman was sharpening his axe, "and there was a horse drinking. After a moment, it looked up at me, flicked its tail, and said 'How many miles to Babylon?'"

"There's no need to be embarrassed," the woodsman said. "You're young. You can't be expected to know the answers to every esoteric question some horse wants to ask you."

"That's not the point," the boy said excitedly. "People will think it strange. Everyone knows that horses don't talk."

"Was this horse wearing a saddle?" the woodsman asked.

"No. I think it was a wild horse," the boy said.

"Then what does it care for the opinions of men?" the woodsman said and turned his attention back to his whetstone.

- 7 -

Here's what Marion did. She did all that stuff you do. She talked to people. She made phone calls. She examined all the relevant paperwork. She pushed and she prodded and she made herself unpopular, kneading at history to try and make a new shape of it. She doubted her sanity often and regretted it hardly at all. And eventually all this doing led her to the complex of buildings where Jonathan had worked and where he had died.

CosmoTech Research had its own grounds on the outskirts of Simi Valley. It had a big rectangular building with very few windows. It had a parking lot and a guard who checked out your legs as you left your car. It had a nifty corporate logo and potted plants in its lobby. What it didn't have was a metal-detector. Which was extremely handy because Marion had a gun.

- 8 -

"Jonathan's alive."

Krevitz blinked, which was a fairly big reaction for him. Marion wasn't sure if she'd in fact ever seen the lids lower on those pale blue eyes before. He preferred to blink when people weren't looking, she'd figured, lest it allow some reading of what he was thinking or feeling. Jonathan and he had known each other since college and they'd already been partnered on their research work when Marion and Jonathan had met. Tidy little man. She'd never liked him and she liked him less now.

His office, surprisingly, wasn't neat and precise—papers and shit were piled everywhere—though there was a completely clear semi-circular area on his desk immediately in front of him as if he was somehow Canuting the tides of chaos and getting a kick out of it. He still hadn't answered her.

"He's alive," she said again. "And you're going to tell me where he is."

"Marion," Krevitz said, "we were both at the funeral."

"Memorial service," Marion said. "You can't have a funeral when there's no body."

"And you can't have a body when a laboratory blows up and everything in it is reduced to ashes."

His voice was as calm as if he were debating a sports scholarship student in a logic class. But then she hadn't shown him the gun yet.

"I have a theory," she said. He smiled a little—as if theories weren't really available to pretty girls who worked in insurance—but she didn't let that put her off. "I think the explosion was a cover. I think your research went further than you ever told anyone. I think you .. you sent him .. somewhere. Somewhere out there."

She was furious with herself for faltering at the end but she couldn't help it. She couldn't say out loud in a sunlit office on an October afternoon in a California suburb what her midnight thoughts had led her to believe: That this privately-financed space research company had somehow built a rocket, launched it in secret, and sent her boyfriend into space.

Krevitz laughed at her, which was all she needed. Her hand was in her purse as he began to speak.

"God almighty, Marion," he said, "Do you honestly think .."

He broke off to stare at the gun.

"Fine," she said. "Fuck what I think. Tell me what happened. Or I swear to Christ I'll shoot you in the face."

- 9 -

She'd made sure they'd walked close together as he led her down to one of the labs, close enough for Krevitz to never stop considering how much damage a bullet could do from such proximity. They'd gone through several levels of security but Krevitz's card had opened every automated door without a problem, despite the satisfying trembling of his hand. By the time he opened the final door they were several stories below ground and hadn't passed another human for quite some time.

The laboratory was probably impressive if you knew anything about laboratories, but, despite her life with Jonathan, Marion had always

KING OF OUTER SPACE

remained happily ignorant of such things. It was a big room full of science shit. She had no idea of the specific functions of most of the equipment with which the place was packed to overflowing - monitors, data-screens, dish-receivers, and a thousand annoyingly untidy wires —but the centerpiece of the whole operation, the thing from which many of those wires originated, was appallingly clear.

An image from a hundred bad movies, it surprised her only in its familiarity: A large vat filled to within a few inches of its glass lip by a salmon-pink translucent substance and, floating in the center of that amniotic jelly, a human brain.

- 10 -

Krevitz's hand was still shaking but the Marlboro seemed to be helping. He was perched on a lab-stool beside a work-bench and was taking long greedy drags of the cigarette as if he still couldn't believe she'd allowed him to light up and might at any moment rescind her permission. As if she cared. As if she cared about anything anymore.

He also wouldn't shut up. Marion doubted he'd ever talked so much in his life. He hadn't actually admitted that he'd killed Jonathan, but his ramblings were making it clear that their relationship had changed in a somewhat fundamental way once Krevitz had realized he needed a guinea-pig.

"He was asleep when it happened," he said. "He didn't feel a thing."

He gestured expansively with his cigarette-free hand at the various data-recording devices.

"He's sending so much stuff," he said, a tiny hint of pride creeping back into his nervous voice, "Stuff a machine just wouldn't get. Guiding intelligence, you see. I knew that was what was needed."

Marion had already started tuning out the specifics. The essence was clear. She'd not really been wrong. Jonathan *was* in space, in a manner of speaking, his mind hardwired into some kind of radio-telescope system and transmitted out into the ether to explore the universe on behalf of this contemptible little shit.

"Does he *know*?" she asked.

Krevitz shook his head.

"We weren't sure," he said, "Until we started getting the pictures."

There was nothing wrong with the VCR or the monitor but the images were distorted and grainy, like a warped kinescope of a weak broadcast of old monochrome nitrate.

"Imagination," said Krevitz. "I hadn't figured on that surviving. But it's allowed him a construct, as you see." He paused, as if puzzled not by the inexplicable presence of the images but by their provenance. "Curious choices."

Of *course* his ship would look like that, Marion thought, Of *course* that's how he'd be dressed. She didn't realize she was weeping until the salt stung her lip.

She let the tears keep coming, crying not for herself but for Jonathan's orphaned consciousness, lost out there in the galaxy and dressing its voyage in half-remembered dreams of space-heroes to comfort its lonely and endless flight.

Her sobbing seemed to increase Krevitz's anxiety. She wasn't surprised. Distraught woman with a gun. Make anyone nervous. She swung to face him, lifting her weapon.

"I can turn it off," he begged, the cigarette dropping from his fingers, "Turn it all off. Give him peace."

Marion let him sweat for a moment, then shook her head.

"That's not what I want," she said.

- 12 -

```
FADE IN

EXT. DEEP SPACE

The ship blasts through the void. Ridiculous.
Magnificent.

DISSOLVE TO

INT. ROCKETSHIP COCKPIT
```

The cabin is identical to when last we saw
it, except that there are now two chairs in
the center.

Jonathan King, astronaut, is in one of them.
In the other, dressed in form-hugging space-
girl gear, is his fellow crew-member. Dale
Arden to his Flash Gordon, Alanna to his Adam
Strange, Dejah Thoris to his John Carter.

Marion looks around the cabin. She blinks ..

.. and the cabin MORPHS in a shimmer of
becoming.

A THRONE-ROOM IN BYZANTIUM -

A royal peacock walks unselfconsciously
behind the enthroned lovers as Marion's
bejewelled hand reaches for Jonathan's.

Jonathan cocks his head, as if learning the
rules of a new game. He blinks ..

A BRIDGE OF A PIRATE'S GALLEON -

The Buccaneer Captain smiles at his Pirate
Princess and lifts his hand to meet hers ..

DISSOLVE TO

EXT. DEEP SPACE

The full-rigged galleon holds its course among
the stars, sails billowing in impossible
winds.

MORPHING in and out of new avatars - a gothic
cathedral, a huge white swan - the ship sails
on, disappearing into the distance.

FADE OUT

DOCTOR ARCADIA

The moon was high when Andrews made the call -
The portrait of her father on the wall
Was bathed in moonlight, Andrews later said
When Nancy wanted details. From her bed
She'd heard the screaming and the curious sound
As of something dragged across the ground,
Something wet and limp and un-intact.
She'd thought at first the dogs had been attacked -
Had pictured wolves, from far across the moors,
Dire and dreadful, breaking through the doors
To savage their emasculated kin
In sight of, and in spite of, screaming Lynne
The parlour-maid - but, waking fully then,
Had realised she'd have to think again.
For this was England, Nineteen Thirty-Three,
And wolves belonged to myth and history.
So what the hell was going on? She'd dressed
And hurried down, found Lynne and Andrews, pressed

Them both for explanations, and been told
"I've made the phone-call, Ma'am. It was the cold
As first alerted me." "The cold?" she'd said
When Andrews paused. The Maid had bobbed her head -
Corroboration of the Butler's point -
"Yeah. *Freezing*, Miss. I felt it in me joint.
The elbow, Miss. Been bad since 'Twenty-Nine.
Was still with Lady Forster then. Been fine
Since working *here*, I..." Nancy'd raised her hand -
She'd heard as much of that as she could stand -
And, turning back to Andrews, asked for more
Information. It was half-past Four
According to the hallway clock, the chime
Of which rang soft and dully, by the time
The Butler led her, Lynne behind them, down
To the Library door. A tiny frown
Crossed Nancy's face. "The door," she said, "is closed".
"Not locked though, Ma'am," the Butler said. Opposed
On principle to closed doors, Nancy sighed,
Reached out her hand to let herself inside,
And, as her fingers curled around the knob,
Heard, beyond the door, a distant throb
Like the engine of a waiting taxi, low
And rhythmic. Nancy cocked her head and, though
The sound itself was surely nothing, still
A curious reluctance stayed her will
And she moved her hand away. Clearing his throat,
Andrews - with an underlying note
Of insistence which he tried his best to hide -
Said "Ma'am, I think you'd better look inside."
The sound she'd thought she heard had disappeared.
Was never there. She'd swallowed, which had cleared
Her head. That's all it was. A ringing in
Her ears. Without a word - Lynne clinging in
Fear to Andrews' arm - she threw the door
Open and led them in. The Library floor

Felt soft beneath her feet. No, not soft. Wet.
Was something moving in the shadows? "Get
A light on!" shouted Lynne, her pallid face
A mask of terror. "Don't forget your place,"
Andrews hissed in anger, "Understand!?"
Lynne nodded, chastened. Nancy, her left hand
Gesturing for silence, used her right
To bathe the room in cold electric light,
Still half-believing it was all a joke.
Walls lined with books on shelves of solid oak.
Bay windows. Leather arm-chairs. Shakespeare's plays
Bound in morocco. Down the countless days
The Library was unchanging. Leather. Wood.
The ghosts of old cigars. And now this. Blood.
Blood everywhere. The floor awash, the walls
Dripping. Smeared across the shelves like scrawls
From some demented artist who chose crime
As canvas and, as medium, viscera. Time
Seemed to freeze for Nancy as she stared
At the scene, as if the present shared
The moment with eternity - a sense
Of *This-Is-Always-So*, a vile offense
To any hope of healing in the soul.
She forced her eyes to focus on a bowl
Of Chinese flowers that sat upon a reading
Table in a corner. As if breeding
Like mutated algae from a foetid
Swamp, the bloody trails originated
From the chair beside the table. No-one sat
There now, of course, but Nancy noticed that
There was a half-drunk glass of scotch upon
The table, strangely undisturbed. "Go on,"
She said to Andrews, pointing at the drink,
"Tell me who was here". "I didn't think,
I really didn't, Ma'am .. I .. "Looking old
And tired, he found his nerve. The tale he told

Confirmed the earlier presence of another:
The unofficial house-guest - Nancy's brother,
Ten years disinherited - had been
Allowed into the house by Andrews, seen
Into the Library, brought a drink, and then
Been left alone at midnight. It was when
The noises started and the sudden cold
Gripped the house that Andrews, fearing old
Enmities between the siblings, rose
To check the situation. "Andrews, close
The door and lock it," Nancy said and led
The servants with her from the room. Lynne said
"Lock it good. I've goosebumps on me skin,"
As Andrews turned the key. "Be quiet, Lynne,"
Nancy said, "We'll stay here in the hall
Until the Police respond to Andrews' call".
"Begging your pardon, Ma'am," the Butler said,
"It weren't the Police I telephoned". Face red
With indignation, Nancy turned to speak
Sharply to him. And then they heard the creak
Of a floorboard from behind the just-locked door.
The three of them all turned to look. Before
Anyone could speak, the light that crept
Through the gap beneath the door was swept
Into a sudden dazzling brightness which
Flickered, pulsed, and then went out. "The switch .. "
Lynne whimpered, half in hope and half in fear.
"I doubt it," Nancy said and, giving the key a
Decisive turn, she pushed the door and then
Re-entered the room, where all was dark again.
Nancy'd read her Christie and her Doyle.
She knew that tainted evidence could foil
A whole investigation. So she'd sought
To isolate the murder scene. She'd thought
The door, once locked, would keep it clean. That was,
It seemed, an insufficient step because -

Tall, forbidding, shadowed in the gloom -
Someone was already in the room.
Lynne clutched at Andrews' arm and screamed in fear.
The Butler shouted, "What're you doing here!?"
The figure, calm and stately, turned its head.
"Forgive me if I startled you," it said,
"I was under the impression I'd been called".
Andrews visibly relaxed. Appalled
And, unlike Andrews, far from calmed, the lady
Of the house looked firmly at the shady
Figure and, while motioning him forward,
Said to him, "*I* didn't call you". "Nor would
Anyone - unless the need was pressing,"
The stranger said, his intonation stressing
Anyone - a thorough implication
That his was not a popular vocation.
He moved a little forward and the moonlight
Caught him. Poor Lynne staggered in a swoon. Night
Personified, the black-clad stranger was
Both striking and mysterious because
The flowing darkness of a full-length cape
Obscured his body's details - though the shape
Hidden within those folds quite clearly hinted
At a powerful presence. Green eyes glinted
From the shadow underneath the brim
Of a black fedora hat. They stared at him.
"Who in God's name are you?" Nancy cried.
"Doctor Arcadia," the man in black replied.
His voice - a low and pleasing baritone -
Was strangely echoed. Like a gramophone
Recording, Nancy thought, heard far away
But loud as normal. Be that as it may,
Nancy looked at him with new respect.
She knew the name, of course, and could connect
The man with certain whispered tales she'd heard.
Problems solved. Discreetly. Cleanly. Word

Had it that the Doctor was the man
Who'd lifted a curse from a Prince of Hindustan.
And the ghost of Heyward Manor - which had scared
Off thirteen priests, three psychics, and a herd
Of curious reporters in a fast
Four weeks - had, in an afternoon, at last
Fallen to Arcadia. He was said
To be the man who'd exorcised the "Red
Baronet" of Surrey in the case
That brought such scandal, not to say disgrace,
On one of England's oldest families
Some years before. The mystery disease
Called in the press *The Death Without A Name* -
Which ravaged half the Orient and came
To England in a cargo-hold and preyed here -
Had claimed no further victims once Arcadia
Had been called in .. Her reverie was shattered
By a cry from Lynne, who pointed at a tattered
Figure by the window who'd appeared
Seemingly from nowhere and who leered
Unpleasantly. No more than four feet high,
And quite disfigured by a milky eye
That wept behind a mottled string of skin,
The figure bowed to each who stood within
The room. "I'd like to introduce you to
My partner," said Arcadia, "Tried and true,
My right hand in both victories and defeats,
This gentleman is my colleague: Mister Sweets".
Barely were the introductions finished
When what little light there was diminished
Even more and all at once a wind
Played about the room. Arcadia grinned
At Mister Sweets and said "I think it's time .. "
Within the darkness, ghostly, in the slime
That the drying blood was turning into,
Something slithered. "Though I can't begin to

Explain why, you must keep extremely still,"
Arcadia told the others. As a thrill
Of fear crept over Nancy's heart, she saw
The thing that slithered had been joined by more
Nebulous shapes in the shadows. Three in all,
They rose, congealing upwards into tall
Dark shapes that writhed in ripples of becoming.
A sense that something even worse was coming
Swept over Nancy and a nascent cry
Escaped her trembling lips, accompanied
By a scream from Lynne. The Doctor paid no heed
To them at all but concentrated solely
On the apparitions. The unholy
Peristaltic things continued growing -
Arms oozing into being, faces showing
Within the shifting darkness of their forms,
Which pulsed and rippled as if teeming swarms
Of insects writhed beneath the skin. The Doctor
Raced to where a table stood. He knocked a
Uniform edition of Jane Austen
To the floor - where all that genteel wit was lost in
Coagulating blood - and hurled the table
Toward the creatures, who were not yet able
To avoid the blow, still rooted as they were
In the blood that birthed them. Watching their
Violent dissolution into poorer
Pieces that fell wriggling to the floor, a
Feeling came to Nancy; not yet calm,
She felt at least a lessening of alarm
And was able to observe with clearer mind
What happened next. As - in an unrefined
And guttural voice - his partner screamed in Latin,
Sweets fell against the chair her brother'd sat in
And all but tumbled to his knees. He gasped,
His face pale and drained of life, and grasped
The chair-leg to support himself. Now what

Was that about - for Sweets was surely not
Arcadia's target? The question fled her mind
As Nancy's eyes swept back across to find
That Sweets was not the only one reacting
To the Doctor's words. The shapes, contracting,
Were bubbling into transmutating matter,
Blossoming into unknown flowers that a
Botanist could only name in nightmare.
As soon as they were formed, those flowers of fright were
Ossified into solid stone. A sound
Accompanied this change that was profound
And dolorous as a mausoleum bell
And, wafting through the room, a hideous smell
Like foetid breath from something's dying gargle
Drifted from the flowers which stood, like marble
Orchids from the fields of the Inferno,
Smoking. Nancy felt her stomach churn. "Oh
God," she said, as the Doctor helped his whey-
Faced partner to his feet, "What on earth were they?"
"Something that should not *be* on earth. A play
Of alien forces sensing disalignment,"
Arcadia said, "And, further, if this sign meant
What I think, then this is far from over.
We'd .. " Andrews interrupted him. "By Jove, a
Job well done, Sir. Very glad I called
You. Frightening as it was, I was enthralled,
I must confess, when you .. " , his voice trailed off
In the face of Arcadia's silent stare, a cough
Covering his confusion. "Mister Sweets?"
The Doctor said, "The ritual completes
Our work on this floor, am I right?" A nod
Came in reply. The Doctor smiled. "How odd,"
He said. He looked at Andrews, then at Lynne,
Then back again, without a word. A thin
And reedy sob escaped Lynne's throat, her eyes
Moist with a sudden knowing sadness. "Lies,"

The Butler murmured, voice unsure and small,
"Lies .." His mistress snapped at Arcadia, "All
You're doing is upsetting them! I demand
To know .." The Doctor raised a silencing hand,
His eyes not leaving Lynne and Andrews. When
He finally spoke, his voice was gentle. "Then
Why are you still here?" he said. The switch
Over by the door, the same one which
Nancy'd used, buzzed audibly. The light
Came back to life. And, blinking out of sight
Like talking-picture characters in a trick
Of the camera, Lynne and Andrews, quick
As that, were gone. And so were all the stone
Flowers and blood. As Nancy gave a moan
Of dread and staggered, riven deep with shock,
Arcadia calmly glanced at the hallway clock
Through the open Library door. "Let's go
Upstairs," he said, "This isn't finished". "No!"
Said Nancy, anger chasing fear away,
"Nobody's going anywhere! We stay
Right here until I know just what the hell
Exactly's going on! You hear me?! Tell
Me what you did to Lynne and Andrews for
A start!" The Doctor moved toward the door
While answering her. "Nothing save remind
Them what they were," he said, "I think you'll find
All your questions answered by the end
Of the night's proceedings. Nancy, I'm a friend.
I'm here to help, I promise. But we must
Move swiftly. Please". Though not exactly trust,
Something in Nancy told her she should do
As Arcadia said. "Then, after you,"
She said to Sweets who nodded, smiling - not
A pretty sight - and led her to the spot
In the hall where Arcadia was standing,
Head tilted to regard the upstairs landing.

They were halfway up the stairs when Nancy thought
Of something she'd forgotten. What had brought
Mister Sweets to his knees in the library? She
Asked the Doctor. "Drawing them out for me
Puts quite a strain on Sweets," he said, "The cost
Of being a Vortex. But we haven't lost
Him yet". He and his partner shared a smile.
"Drawing them out?" said Nancy, puzzled. "While
The kind of problem people call us for
Might naturally be disturbing to them, more
Often than not the manifestation's merely
Hinting at itself and isn't nearly
Ripe for exorcism," Arcadia said,
"To lance a boil, you bring it to a head".
"And that's where Sweets comes in?" said Nancy. "Right,"
The Doctor said, "A nexus for both Light
And Dark and all the forces in between,
He lets me see the things that can't be seen".
"Let me get this straight. He gives his trust,"
Nancy said, mouth twisted in disgust,
"And you use him as *bait*?" Arcadia, voice
Quite free of guilt, said "Yes. It's not our choice
But Mister Sweets, one could say, is the cheese".
"And the trap is .. ?" Nancy asked. "My expertise,"
The Doctor answered, turning down the landing.
Moments later, finding herself standing
Staring at her bedroom's tight-shut door,
Nancy frowned. "It wasn't closed before,"
She said, "*I* didn't close it". "No. You close
A door extremely rarely. One of those
Little habits people have," the Doctor
Said, "Am I right?" Arcadia's guess unlocked a
Strange sensation in Nancy's heart, despite
His easy off-hand tone. Her throat was tight.
She suddenly felt a chilling rush of fear
And, for a heartbeat only, seemed to hear

An echoed sound like distant beating oars
Through alien seas off unimagined shores.
Arcadia opened the door and led them in.
Nancy hardly noticed that Sweets' skin
Was dotted with sudden sweat because her eyes
Were riveted elsewhere. Although the size
And shape were right and it looked like her bed
Was where she'd left it, Nancy gasped with dread.
Her bedroom was a portrait in decay.
Mildew, cobwebs, peeling paint. A grey
Sheen over everything. Stains on the walls,
Sheets rancid with neglect. Tiny dustballs
Skittering over the buckling floorboards. "No!"
Cried Nancy, sobbing with dismay. "Let's go,"
Arcadia said to Sweets, his voice a mix
Of pity and urgency, "Quickly. Get a fix.
I think we should be somewhere else for this".
Traceries swept over Nancy's face like the kiss
Of a thousand breeze-borne blossoms as the space
Around them shivered into ribbons of place
And moment, both without a meaning. Either
Centuries or inches passed by, neither
Mile nor minute mattering. Eventually,
The sense of movement ceasing, Time could be
Time again and Nancy came around.
The ocean smell hit her first and then the sound
Of breaking waves against the great ship's hull.
A starry sky was overhead. A lull
In the ocean's music let her hear the tinkling
Of glasses from a cocktail bar. An inkling
Of where she was came to her. Strings of fairy
Lights coloured the deck. "It's the Queen Mary,"
She said to Arcadia, who she realised now
Was standing close beside her, "Doctor, how
Did we .. ", "Mister Sweets," he interrupted,
While a drunken mix of laughter and shouts erupted

From a lower deck. "Where is he?" Nancy
Asked. Arcadia shrugged and smiled. "I fancy
He's stealing a drink somewhere. He'll be along
By and by," he said, "I get a strong
Impression that you know this ship". A smile
Blossomed on Nancy's face which charmed him while
She answered. "*Everybody* knows this ship,"
She said and looked round with delight, "A trip
To New York on the Queen is the *only* way
To sail this season". In order to watch the play
Of the moonlight on the waves, she moved and leant
Her elbows on the rail. As if it meant
A great deal, he asked her "Nancy, what year
Is this?" She pointed out across the sea. A
Shooting star was falling to the water.
"Look!" she cried excitedly, "We oughtta
Make a wish! I'd be a mermaid. Swim
Forever!" Then she turned and looked at him.
"What year?" she said, "It's Nineteen Thirty-Three.
Why'd you ask me?" Saying nothing, he
Looked out at the ocean. Nancy smiled.
"How beautiful it is," she said, beguiled,
"There's only music missing now, you know".
As if she'd cued it, drifting from below,
Echoed and poignant, came the sound of the band
Playing *I'll Follow My Secret Heart*. "I stand
Corrected," Nancy said, "I love this song.
I always have". She almost sang along.
"Noel Coward sails, I understand.
Has he heard them play, I wonder? And
Did he like their version?" Arcadia looked
Back at her. She shivered. He unhooked
His cape and wrapped it round her. When he spoke,
His voice was very careful. As the smoke
From the three great funnels disappeared
Against the cloudless star-filled sky, he cleared

His throat. "The song's from Nineteen Thirty-Four,"
He said, "Which was a good two years before
This ship's maiden voyage, by the way".
Nancy looked confused. "What did you say?"
She said, her voice a small and frightened thing.
Her hands flew to her shoulders as if to cling
To a self she suddenly felt unsure of.
"Mister Sweets, you see, has opened the door of
Dreams," Arcadia said, an obvious sorrow
In his voice. "I'm dreaming of Tomorrow?"
Nancy asked him. But he shook his head.
"You have no tomorrows," the Doctor said,
"This is a dream of the life you might have had".
Nancy trembled. Not afraid but sad.
Profoundly sad. A sadness too deep for tears.
"Help me .. " she whispered, "Help me. All those years .. "
As unbidden images ricocheted in her mind,
Arcadia's voice grew confident and kind.
"We've played a game of the soul, dear, you and me.
Or - as the French would say - a *jeu d'esprit*.
But now the game is over and it's time
To send you home. Farewell to pantomime,
Goodbye to make-believe. Look at the sky".
Nancy tipped her head. She gasped. A sigh
Of wonder fled her mouth. She felt her knees
Tremble like the knees of one who sees
Something long imagined and long yearned-for
In the soul. A memory that burned. For
Overhead, like home-shores seen at last,
Beyond the stars, the sky was dancing. Vast
Coruscating sheets of shimmering light,
Translucent, multi-coloured, filled the night.
Nancy gasped, delight and awe competing
In her soul and in her wildly beating
Heart. "That is your home," Arcadia said,
His voice dim in her ears. She turned her head,

Feeling she should say goodbye before ..
But she couldn't really see him anymore.
She felt her flesh dissolve, her spirit shed ..
In time to see his partner tilt his head
To the sky to watch the closing of the case,
Mister Sweets arrived on deck, his face
Pale and sweating from the strain of holding
All of them in the Dream Country. "The enfolding
Is complete," the Doctor said, "The Colourfield
Has her". The Queen Mary's sirens pealed
Their thunderous note, a *basso profundo* A.
The Doctor murmured "Let's be on our way".

Five-fifteen. God. Up all fucking night
Again. Ralph Mannering stood up, killed the light,
Slipped another DVD inside
The player, hit the surround-sound, and then tried
Yet again to keep his mind from dwelling
On the night's business. Mostly he'd been telling
Family and colleagues he was getting
Some work done on the place and wasn't letting
Anyone visit till the work was through.
Come to think of it, that was really true -
It was the *nature* of the work he didn't care
To tell them. Didn't care. Or wouldn't dare.
He could imagine Jeremy Bentley's face on hearing
He'd spent hard cash on shit like this. An earring
And a face tattoo'd go better. Instant doom
For business cred. Ralph looked around the room.
It used to be a Library, he recalled,
Before he'd had the screening room installed
And banked the floor to face the 60-incher.
His thoughts turned to his realtor. He could lynch her.
Cheerfully. God knows, imagined violence
Was fair exchange for the bitch's careful silence

Re Garwood Grange's live-in apparition.
He'd never been a one for superstition
Before he bought the place. But now he'd been
Converted. Couldn't count the times he'd seen
The scared, confused, and bloodied female ghost
That plagued his house. What pissed him off the most
Was the fear she'd manifest herself in front
Of business contacts - Christ, the little cunt
Had cost him thousands on an Asian sale
Just last weekend. He couldn't afford to fail,
Not with this mortgage. God, it made him sick.
He hoped the men he'd hired could do the trick.
They'd blinked out of his sight about an hour
Ago - how weird was *that* - but still, more power
To them if it got the job done. Who
Cared how they did it or what they looked like. Screw
Appearances. As long as they could earn
Their money. A sound behind him made him turn.
"Your house is clean again," the Doctor said.
Ralph, surprised to see them, cocked his head.
"Christ, you've not been gone long," he said, "Did
It give you any trouble? Are we rid
Of it?" "Of *It*?" the Doctor said. "The ghost".
"Her name was Nancy," Arcadia told his host,
"And in this room two servants and she were slain
By her brother. He didn't hang. Insane,
The Judge decided. Institutionalised
Since 1933, he's recognised
By few of those who have him in their care
As dangerous. In fact, his nurses swear
He's nothing other than a sweet old man
Of ninety-seven. Time does what it can
To ease .. " Ralph cut him off, "Whatever. She
Gone for good?" The Doctor sighed. "I see
No more problems. She'd heard of me. I believe
That helped," he said. Unable to conceive

How that was possible, Ralph was confused
But did his best to keep his voice amused.
"Heard of you?" he asked, "How old are you?"
The Doctor said "I'm nearly forty-two."
He paused and shrugged, "And have been for some time."
The clock outside the library gave a chime.
As if on cue, beyond the window, came
The dawn's first light, a tiny band of flame
Low on the horizon. Birds began to sing
Outside the house. From somewhere came a ring.
"The telephone," Arcadia said, "Will be
My agent ready to discuss my fee."
The phone was near the doorway to the hall
And Ralph moved across the room to take the call.
Mister Sweets stared after him for a second
Or two, glanced round the room as if something beckoned
To him from beyond its walls, then, looking
Up at the Doctor, his expression brooking
No argument, he turned and spat on the floor.
Arcadia looked over to the door
Where Ralph, his back to them, was on the phone.
"Perhaps we should leave Mr Mannering alone,"
He said. As Sweets summoned up an Interface
To smoothly fold them both through time and space,
His partner took a moment to nod his head.
"I liked her better, too," Arcadia said.

INTRICATE GREEN FIGURINES

*But the things on his mantel—I dare not describe
them—encouraged my early exit from that place.*
– from a letter to E. F. Benson by Thomas St. John Bartlett.

Well, he wasn't the best drummer we'd ever heard, he was definitely on the wrong side of thirty, and he was, you know, a fucking coke dealer.

On the other hand, he had a big house in which we could rehearse for free, his girlfriend Sylvie had amazing legs, and he was, you know, a coke dealer. Besides, we had a gig coming up in three day's time and nobody else had bothered to answer the ad. So that was how Joey Galligan joined the band.

How he left it was a bit more complicated.

They found him nailed to his wall one Sunday morning. Funny story. Joey was an analog-snob—didn't own a single CD, it was wall to wall LPs and 45s—and it was one of the clichéd drawbacks of vinyl that made the neighbor lady finally call the Police. The needle had got stuck in the groove of "Accidents will Happen"—which was bizarre to begin with because Joey fucking *hated* Elvis Costello—and Mrs. Adams, doing her best to get breakfast going for the kids, was being driven out of her mind by the nonstop reiteration of *rise up in the sweat and smoke like/rise up in the sweat and smoke like/rise up in the sweat and smoke like.* She had a reasonably good idea of how that nice young Galligan fellow made the bulk of his money and, not being by nature a snitch, she'd tried to do the right thing first—called Joey's number several times and got the machine, even sent little Derek round to hammer on the door—but there are limits to a housewife's patience. The coppers found a back window unlatched and, not too long after, found Joey. It took the Coroner a couple of days of heavy pondering to finally return a verdict of murder by person or persons unknown—must've figured suicide was, you know, a bit of a stretch—but eventually the body was released for burial.

Even though it was late September, the sun had come out after the morning rain and—in contrast to the grey misery of the service – the interment itself looked like it'd been dressed and lit by professionals; mist steaming off the rich green of the cemetery lawns and sunlight glinting on the golden letters of the neighboring epitaphs.

"Thanks for coming, Tony," Sylvie said, as the first shovelful of soil hit the coffin. I hadn't noticed her move away from the priest to stand next to me. She'd selected her wardrobe for appropriate reasons of mourning, I'm sure, and she was doing a halfway decent job of not letting anyone see how fully aware she was that she looked fucking great in black.

"Nice shades," I said.

She flicked a strand of blonde hair away from the surfer-style Ray-bans in acknowledgement. "Thanks," she said. "Nice suit. You should wear that at your gigs." Joey'd been with us for almost four months by then and Syl had never been bashful about her opinion that the whole band could benefit from a prolonged session with a stylist.

"Yeah, but it's me sister's boyfriend's," I said. "I don't think he'd appreciate the sweat stains."

She grinned. "Anyway," she said, "I was wondering if I could have a word with you?"

"What about?" I said, which I understand might strike you as somewhat lacking in grace given the circumstances but I still wasn't completely convinced that her trip down to London the weekend Joey'd been killed had been entirely coincidental.

She looked over to the handful of other mourners—couple of fellow musicians, a few civilian friends, no-one from the world of Joey's other income-stream—and chewed fetchingly on her lower lip. "Not here," she said.

The pub was on Lime Street. It wasn't really called The Big House but for nearly a century that had been the only name anybody in Liverpool had ever used for it. It was just a block away from the Adelphi Hotel—the upscale bars of which I'd've thought were more Syl's speed, but whatever—and my taxi got me there a good five minutes before hers did.

She came in carrying a thin briefcase, which she hadn't had at the cemetery and which probably explained the delay. Probably explained her suggestion of separate cabs, too. I had a scotch-and-coke waiting for her and she took a courtesy sip before getting down to business. She laid the briefcase on the table and popped its catches, but looked at me before actually opening it.

"I need your advice," she said.

"Alright," I said, shrugging to suggest that, while I was perfectly willing to offer advice, I couldn't guarantee that it would be of any use.

"Joey left these to me." She nodded at the still unopened briefcase.

Joey—who'd turned thirty-three on his last birthday—had never really struck me as the type to have prepared a Last Will and Testament.

"Left them to you?" I said, and gave her a look.

She gave me one back. "He'd have wanted me to have them." Butter wouldn't melt.

We deadpanned each other for a moment or two, but the second her smile started I smiled right back. Because here's the thing; if you met Syl, you'd love her. Everybody did. Funny. Gorgeous. Foul-mouthed. What's not to like? You just had to be aware that she had an admirably Malcolm X attitude toward her particular routes of escape from the

71

Liverpool gutters; By Any Means Necessary. And I had no argument with that. So she might have helped herself to some goodies from Joey's worldly remains, goodies that weren't strictly hers for the taking. So the fuck what? It certainly wasn't going to do Joey any harm now.

"Let's have a look, then," I said.

Syl lifted the lid, turning the case on the table so that it was facing me. "Do you think they're worth money?"

At some stage, the case had been fitted with a specially designed display mounting of pale leather. Set into it, in three rows of three, were nine small hollows, each of them about an inch deep. Three of the hollows were empty and the other six were each occupied by a small carved figure in a semi-translucent green stone.

I was getting quite good at shrugging. "Got to be worth *something*," I said. "Not a full set, though." I gestured at the three empty spaces.

"You think that matters?"

"Well, of course it matters," I said, basing this expert opinion on the time I'd been sneered at by some tosser behind the counter at a comic-book shop for trying to sell him a bunch of *Star Wars* bubble-gum cards that were apparently compromised to the point of geek-world disdain because they didn't include the Boba Fett sub-set. "But it doesn't mean that they're not still valuable."

"They *look* valuable," Syl said. "Do you think they're chess pieces?"

I pointed at the hollows again. "There's *nine* of them."

"Alright, smart-arse," she said. "What are they, then?"

"I've no idea." I picked one of the little carvings up for a closer look. It was heavier than I expected. The workmanship was really impressive, especially given its small size, and I tried to imagine the eye and the tools—and the fucking *patience*—needed to carve something so exquisite.

The Big House had never served a bad pint in its life, but as I turned the little figurine so that its greenness caught and held the light, I suddenly felt like the bitter was souring in my stomach.

"Are they all this nasty?" I said, squinting at it. It was a guy with goat's legs—a faun, if I was remembering my old Narnia books properly—and its bare chest was studded with arrows and its tiny bearded face frozen in agony.

"Fucking right they are," said Syl, and picked out another to hand to me. "Check out *this* poor cow." It was a mermaid who was holding her severed head between her naked breasts. At first glance I'd thought she was weeping but looking more closely I saw that her eyes had been put out and that what I'd taken for tears were actually minuscule drops of blood.

My beer was definitely losing its taste. I put the little green horrors back in their respective hollows and looked back at their latest owner. "I don't know what to tell you, Syl," I said. "I mean, I agree with you, they'd have to fetch a good price *somewhere* but, you know, what the fuck can *I* do about it? You'd have to take them to some kind of proper appraiser, someone who knows what the hell they're talking about. Castle Street's got a bunch of fancy Antique dealers. Try some of them."

She gave me a look that managed to be both help-me-I'm-a-damsel-in-distress and Oh-Christ-I'm-drinking-with-an-idiot, which was quite a trick. But I saw her point.

"Joey got them from a customer?" I said.

"I've no idea, Tony," she said, and was kind enough not to sigh. "But I think it's a fair fucking bet, don't you?"

"Yeah, but it still doesn't mean they were nicked. I mean, Joey's clientele wasn't *all* crack-heads and dole-ites, was it? Half the fucking barristers in Bold Street bought their blow from him. I saw the twat that did me Mum's divorce round his place once."

"Doesn't matter though, does it?" she said. "Even if it *was* some lawyer who'd had them, they'd tell the filth they were stolen before they'd say they were traded for a couple of baggies."

"Yeah, alright," I said, acknowledging that perhaps legitimate dealers were not after all the appropriate market for her sick little treasures. I reached over and closed the briefcase. "But I still don't know what good you think I can do."

"You went to University, Tony," she said. "You must have some posh mates. You know, art collectors or whatever."

"So you don't really want my *advice*, then," I said. "You want me to sell them for you."

"Well, put out some feelers, is all," she said, and treated me to one of her best smiles. "I'll do the actual selling. You're on for ten percent

73

finder's fee. Come on, Tone. Find me somebody rich and stupid who hasn't had his knob sucked for years. One look at me and he'll pay a couple of hundred over the odds."

She'd never lacked for confidence, our Syl. Nor, in that area at least, had she ever had reason to. I gave a tentative nod. "There's one or two blokes I could call, I suppose."

"Great," she said, and clicked the catches shut on the briefcase.

"Hang on," I said. "There's something I need to be clear on."

"What?"

I tapped the briefcase. "Do these have anything to do with Joey being killed?"

"How do you mean?"

"I mean, he wasn't killed *for* them, was he?"

"Well, if he was, they didn't find them."

"Oh," I said. "And you find that reassuring, do you?"

"Oh fuckoff, Tony," she said, like I was just being a dick. "You want in on this or not?"

I let her wait for a beat or two. You know, just being a dick. "Alright," I said. "I'll give you a bell if I get any bites."

"Cheers," she said, and stood up. She took the briefcase and turned to go.

"Syl?"

She turned back to look at me.

"Sincere condolences on your loss."

"Piss off," she said, not without affection, and left.

Thing is, there actually *was* someone I knew who I thought might be interested in what Syl had to offer. Interested in the figurines, at least—Patrick was unlikely to be swayed by the bonus of Syl's physical appeal unless his sexual tastes had done a one-eighty in the last few weeks—so I nipped round to see him.

Long story short. He asked me a lot of questions and showed me a lot of reference books and, after I'd cut him off midway through some fucking lecture about *fin-de-siecle* symbolists incorporating Ming dynasty aesthetics into their work, he dug out a checkbook—I'd explained

Syl probably wasn't set up for plastic—and waited impatiently while I phoned her and told her we were coming. I'd've found some coded way of telling her not to bother getting all vamped up for this particular customer, but she had somebody ringing her doorbell and hung up on me before we could get into it.

The street was a slow curving promenade along the open side of Sefton Park and the three-storey redbrick Victorians that lined it had been built as family homes back when Liverpool still had families that could afford homes of that size. The houses had long been converted to flats, of course, but you couldn't tell that from the outside and walking the street on an autumn night—with its widely-spaced Victorian lamp-posts and its pavement full of fallen leaves blown in from the park—could still make you feel like maybe you'd stepped back into the past. How Syl had managed to scam herself a ground-floor three-bedroom there didn't bear thinking about, though my default assumption involved some hapless Managing Director now safely back with the wife and kids somewhere on The Wirral and still wondering just what the fuck had hit him.

Patrick and I had crossed the park from his place in Mossley Hill and were walking along the street toward Syl's building, Patrick actively crunching the leaves beneath his feet with all the unselfconscious glee of a seven year old.

"'Neath hollow hills, the screaming stone/is carved by idle children's hands," he said in sing-song, timing his leaf-crushing to the rhythm of the words.

"Very nice, Patrick," I said. "But we've already got a lyricist."

He laughed. "Not mine," he said. "Just some doggerel from one of Arthur Symons' less talented friends."

"More of your Eighteen Nineties shit?" I said. Thing about Patrick was that he'd made a fucking fortune by selling a ridiculous dotcom business just before the bubble burst and was now pretty much fully occupied by spending it on acquiring things that could help him pretend the twentieth century had never happened. I don't think he'd actually developed an absinthe habit yet but if you've got a bottle lying around I could probably get you a good price.

I think we heard the laughter before we saw them.

It drifted back toward us, carried on the breeze, a gentle and musical ripple of quiet delight, and we both looked up.

The third lamppost ahead was directly outside the garden gate of the house containing Syl's flat. The two lampposts in between were both dead, leaving a twenty or thirty yard stretch of darkness between us and the pavement outside the gate. Lights being on the blink in suburban Liverpool wasn't exactly unusual but in this particular case it couldn't help but lend a certain air of spot-lit theatricality to what we saw.

Emerging from the gate and into that single pool of warm orange light were three figures, two men and a woman. It was the woman whose laughter we'd heard and she was still laughing as the older of the two men, heavy-set and white-haired, held the gate open for her. The other man—very slightly built and holding a decorative silver-topped walking cane in one gloved fist as if ready to twirl it like a majorette's baton—was the first to look back down the street and see us. He didn't appear to say anything to his companions but the second he registered us the woman's laughter stopped and all three of them, after turning to face us, stopped moving and stood still beneath the lamplight. The older man was holding Syl's briefcase in front of his ample stomach.

Patrick and I stopped too, without either of us really knowing what for. Well, that's bollocks, of course; we stopped because we didn't want to get any closer to them. Fuck knows why—old fat guy, girl, and a midget—but, trust me, keeping our distance felt like the right thing to do.

Their faces remained expressionless as they stared back at us but I still got the feeling that they were *choosing* to let us see them, and taking some mysterious pleasure in it. The streetlight washed most of the color out of them but the woman's hazel eyes glinted green as a small smile returned to her painted mouth. The little dandy with the stick raised a single amused eyebrow at us and then turned his head to the older man as if waiting to be told what to do. I thought of a terrier eager to be let off its leash, and immediately wished I hadn't.

"Are they wearing *make-up*?" Patrick said, very quietly.

He might have been right, though it was difficult to be sure. There was an unsettling gleam to the skin of all three faces as if the lamplight was catching a grease base within their pallor.

The fat man still hadn't responded to his friend's silent enquiry but, after letting another long few seconds go by, he inclined his head slightly in a gestural bow and, without a word, all three of them turned and walked away out of the lamppost's circle of light.

Patrick and I didn't say anything to each other but I was touched and impressed that, once I started walking towards Syl's gate again, he didn't fuckoff and leave me to it.

The front door of the house had been left latched but unlocked and so had the door to Syl's flat. We let ourselves in. All the lights had been turned off and the curtains drawn and the fact that I called Syl's name as I fumbled blindly to find the switch for the overhead was more about me wanting to feel that everything was normal than about expecting an answer.

Something whistled in the darkness and I heard Patrick jump back against the wall in shock. My fingers finally found the switch and the second the light was on we both realized the whistling, rising in pitch and intensity, was just Syl's kettle reaching boiling point.

"Fuck. Turn that off, will you?" I said to Patrick, nodding in the direction of the kitchen. I remembered the stuck record in Joey's house and wondered if after all it had been a willful signal that there was something waiting to be found.

The flat was completely undisturbed. As, at first glance, was Syl herself. She was perched on a high stool in front of her counter, posed as if ready for an at-home photo shoot. The work her visitors had done had been done with precision and the area thoroughly cleaned of stains or splashes. Syl's face bore no trace of violence and it was only with a second look that the countless tight black stitches holding her dismembered body together became apparent.

THE CUBIST'S ATTORNEY

Thing is, he hadn't even liked the guy. Only met him once. Fifteen years ago, and the little prick must have been over eighty then. He'd been one of the other guests at a soiree of Doug Gordon's and, even for Doug's crowd of narcissistic mediacrats, Gabriel Anzullar had seemed to be more than somewhat full of himself.

Demanding attention and delivering aphorisms that sounded not only rehearsed but dusty with long service, he'd monopolized several party conversations – which God knows were dull enough in the first place – with cobwebbed stories of his time in the sun. He'd been a minor painter in a time of giants and, his more talented and more famous colleagues having done him the kindness of dying before him, he could command center stage now simply because he'd survived them all. And that seemed to be a perfectly sufficient reason for many of the other guests at the party to hover around him adoringly. To spend time with him wasn't a brush with greatness exactly, but it was at least a brush with one who had brushed.

Jackson himself, spectacularly uninterested in Anzullar's tales of post-war Paris and nineteen-fifties New York, had exchanged maybe three sentences with the old man. Nothing significant – *Paté's good, huh?*, *Yes, have you tried the squab?*, shit like that – and, after the third, Anzullar had turned to their hostess – Doug's third wife, the anorexic blonde – and asked her, as if teasing out some special secret, "And what does our young friend here do for a living?"

The wife – Margaret, was it? Some piss-elegant version of that anyway. Margaux, that was it – had paused for a second and looked at Jackson as if trying to remember. He took pity on her and answered for himself.

"I'm a lawyer," he said.

"Oh!" Anzullar said, "A *lawyer*."

He'd stressed the word into a ridiculous burlesque of a man overwhelmingly impressed. It was like Jackson had told him he was the guy who'd invented water or gravity or something.

"Do you have a card?" he'd asked as if both the possibility was slim and the audacity of the request breathtaking. Jackson had handed one over and then the tides of the party had taken them both elsewhere.

He hadn't thought about him at all in the decade and a half since then. Hadn't even read past the first paragraph of the *Times* obituary last week.

But now the widow had called and asked him in his capacity as her late husband's attorney to contact the heirs and read the will. Jackson's attempts to tell her that he'd never actually become Anzullar's lawyer were met with a somewhat offended directness. "Well, he gave me your *card*," she'd said, as if that was that.

And apparently it was, because Jackson had found himself agreeing to take receipt of the will. He wasn't sure exactly what had prompted his why-the-hell-not response. Maybe it was a slow day. Maybe he hadn't wished to upset a recently-bereaved woman, however pissy she was. Maybe he just figured it would make for a fine dinner-party story, one that needed the third act of the actual reading of the will to make its little drama complete. All he knew was that now, with the document actually lying on his desk in front of him, he wished he hadn't been so stupidly amenable. He took another quick glance at it.

Christ, he had to read this shit with a straight face?

It wasn't a will. Not in any sense other than the formal and the clumsy layman's attempt at legalese that opened it. It was more like Anzullar had decided to make this document his last work of art, albeit literary rather than pictorial. Perhaps he thought it was clever. Jackson begged to differ. It was precious and twee and would stand up to any legal challenge about as long as a hard-on in the proximity of a straight razor.

He glanced at his desk-clock.

Three twenty-nine.

The recipients of Anzullar's largesse would be here any moment. He hoped they were bringing their senses of humor.

As if prompted by his very thought of them, the beneficiaries entered his office and sat down. There were three of them and they were absolutely identical.

Jackson had met twins before and knew of course that triplets existed – but there was something really disturbing about staring across his desk at what appeared to be three editions of exactly the same person. It might conceivably have been less disconcerting if the person in question had been – what? An ugly middle-aged guy running to fat and losing his hair? – but what was sitting in triplicate in his room was a stunningly beautiful young woman.

They were the daughters, or so the widow – who was not herself named in the will and was thus not herself present – had told him. Jackson realized now, with a rush of reluctant admiration for the recently departed old bugger, that Anzullar must not only have scored himself quite the hot young chick for his second wife but also have managed to impregnate her sometime in his mid-seventies, because these girls – girl? girl cubed? – couldn't have been more than twenty-one years old.

And gorgeous. Absolutely drop-dead gorgeous.

The three sisters each tipped their head a little to the side in a gesture of inquiry and gentle puzzlement and Jackson realized that he'd been staring at them for several seconds without saying a word.

Gathering his professionalism as best he could, he spoke up, his voice polite and clear and mercifully free of overt lust.

"Thank you all for coming," he said. "My sincere condolences for your loss. I'm Isaac Jackson."

81

"Chinchilla," said the first daughter.

"Diamante," said the second.

"Sam," said the third.

Hmm. Perhaps Anzullar's copy of *The Poseur's Guide to Naming One's Children* had been missing the entries for 'S'. Whatever. Jackson gave them all a respectable smile and then picked up their father's will.

A whole page was devoted to the single phrase *Clause the First* written in magenta ink by a spidery hand that was presumably the deceased's own. The following page contained said clause, and Jackson read it aloud just as if it had been written by someone less full of shit.

"To the worms of the earth and other agents of decay I leave all my worldly goods. May their desiccation, liquefaction, ossification, and putrefaction be found sportive to those with eyes to see."

Chinchilla gave a brief musical laugh.

Sam clapped her hands once in delight.

"Oh, Daddy," said Diamante, in that tone of disapproving affection that people use for their mischievous but beloved children or outrageous but adored friends.

Jackson felt an obligation to clarify things for them. "We can assume your father means to let his house and possessions stand and rot," he said. "While that may be his wish, it's certainly something you could seek to overturn on the grounds of --"

Chinchilla interrupted him. "You mean claim his *house*?" she said.

"His *things*?" said Sam. "*I* don't want them. Do *you* want them?" she asked her sisters.

"No," said Diamante, and Chinchilla shook her head.

"Okay," said Jackson. "Moving on."

Clause the Second, equally cavalier in its generous waste of paper, was the first of the bequests to the girls.

"To my precious Diamante," Jackson read aloud, "I give the following observation. May she use it wisely.

"When the philosopher-poet Bob Marley said *Don' worry 'bout a thing. Every little thing's gonna be alright*, do you honestly think he was lying?"

That was it. Jackson looked up apologetically at Diamante and was astonished to see that her eyes had misted with tears.

Sam reached her hand over and squeezed her sister's.

"I'm so happy for you," Chinchilla said, as Diamante nodded her thanks.

Jackson did his best to keep his face benignly blank as he looked at them. Jesus Christ. All three of them. Beautiful. Arousing. And as barking mad as their fucking father. He turned his attention back to the will.

"To my adored Sam," he read, "I leave the afternoon of September the seventh, Nineteen-sixty-three, as it appeared in New Brighton, England between the hours of two and five. I also grant her full custody of the adjectives *crepuscular* and *antediluvian*. I trust to her generosity of spirit that she will not unnecessarily withhold their fair usage by others."

Sam seemed as delighted by her inheritance as Diamante had been with hers, whispering her adjectives repeatedly under her breath as Jackson turned to Clause the Third.

"To my beloved Chinchilla, I bequeath the following air:"

Jackson paused there. That single sentence at the top of the page was followed only by a hand-drawn musical staff which contained the notes of a melody spread out over eight measures. The rest of the page was blank.

"I'm afraid I can't read music," Jackson said, and held the page out uncertainly to Chinchilla. She took it eagerly and, holding it to her face, seemed to smell it. No, more than that, really. Seemed almost to breathe it in. After a moment, she held the loose leaf out so that her sisters could see.

"How *generous*!" said Sam, with a pleasure apparently untainted by envy.

"Do you .. do you know the tune?" Jackson asked, feeling like an idiot.

Chinchilla nodded. "It's a melody from the Italian," she said. "The words tell of how Harlequin came to the shores of a great salt lake and burned the still-beating heart of his lost love."

There was a suitably impressed silence for a moment, which was broken by a braying snort from Diamante. "No it's *not*," she said. "It was written on Daddy's piano by that awful little man from Cedar

Rapids. It was a jingle. For a *product*. Metamucil or something equally banal."

"Diamante, you are so fucking *literal*," Chinchilla said. "I'm not sure you're my sister at all. I'm really not."

Chinchilla laid the piece of paper back down on Jackson's desk and looked at him.

"Thank you for your time, Mister Jackson," she said. "Are we done here?"

Jackson hesitated for a second. "Um .. No. Not quite. This is a little awkward." He glanced down at the final page of the will. "I'll just read the last Clause, shall I?"

"Please," said Sam, encouragingly.

Jackson cleared his throat. "To Isaac Jackson, for services rendered, I leave a gift which will be given to him at a time and place of my daughters' choosing."

The girls were silent for a moment. A look passed between Chinchilla and Sam, and then Chinchilla looked back at Jackson.

"Oh, yes. Yes," she said. "I know about that. I'll be in touch." Her mood seemed to have been ruined a little by her earlier disagreement with Diamante. Not sad or annoyed, really. More distracted. She stood up, gesturing to her sisters to do the same.

Jackson stood too, sweeping the pages of Anzullar's will back together and putting them in a file folder. Sam shook his hand. Diamante did the same. They headed for the door, leaving Chinchilla standing by Jackson's desk. After she too had shaken his hand and repeated her thanks, he nodded down at the file.

"Technically, the page with the melody on it is your inheritance," he said. "Your physical property. If you'll let me Xerox a copy for the files, you could take it now."

"No need," she said.

"Okay. If you're sure," he said. "I should point out, by the way, that if your sister is correct, you own *only* the piece of paper. You can't really do anything with the tune. Commercially, I mean. The copyright remains with the composer or his publisher."

Chinchilla smiled at him.

"You misunderstand," she said. "My father hasn't left me the copyright. Nor that piece of paper. He has left me the melody itself."

She leaned in and whispered in his ear. "And with it I can unlock the world."

Jackson eased the Maserati up to 70 and flicked on the cruise control. The road was so straight and so uncongested that he felt he could probably even prop the *Times* against the steering wheel and take another crack at the crossword but he resisted the temptation. Instead, he pushed the radio pre-sets until he found something he remembered from his college days and then sat back and let Tom Petty explain how American girls were raised on promises.

Over to the west, the sun was setting. Jackson turned off the AC and cracked the windows a little to let in the evening's gathering breeze. The odometer said he'd been traveling thirteen miles since he'd turned off the county road onto the state highway. Shouldn't be far now.

He hadn't expected to ever hear from Chinchilla or her sisters again, and had given little thought to the unspecified gift that he was supposed to receive. What was it likely to be anyway? Custody of all oblique angles found in geometry textbooks published between 1921 and 1934? Part-ownership of the color green? Gimme a fucking break.

But a few days after their first meeting Chinchilla had called. Her voice on the phone had been warm and inviting and Jackson had found himself inevitably wondering while she spoke if there was any possibility at all that the gift she was to give him would involve her being naked and pliant. He was way too old to be led by his dick anymore but he'd nevertheless found himself writing down certain coordinates and travel instructions and agreeing to meet.

And now here he was. On the road. Like a hormone-drenched high-schooler kicked into gear by a kiss and a whisper.

He'd thought he was familiar with this stretch of highway but the lines of strip malls and outlet stores that he'd expected to run all the way to the merge with the Interstate had long since disappeared behind him and all that was visible now on either side of the road was flat grassland, its colors already fading into a uniform deep purple as the sun finally dipped out of sight beyond the low and distant western hills.

A black limousine hurtled past on the other side of the divider line heading back to civilization. Jackson watched its tail-lights disappear in his rear-view and realized it was the only other vehicle he'd seen in either direction for several minutes. He also realized that the breeze coming in through his windows had dropped several degrees once the sun had vanished. He didn't need to put the heater on yet but he rolled up the windows and wondered again why the hell he was doing this.

Chinchilla's instructions, needless to say, had kept up the family tradition. Why use street names or freeway numbers when there was a whole world of latitudes, longitudes, north-by-northwests, and Evening Stars to play with? And the meeting point wasn't specified so much as poetically alluded to. He'd managed to translate it down to this highway at least and asked her if he'd reach the Interstate. She'd said no and, when he asked where he turned off, added that he needn't turn off, that he'd stop when it was appropriate, and that she'd be there. He took that to mean that somewhere between here and the Interstate – theoretically just a mile or so ahead, though he could see no sign of it yet despite the flat ribbon of highway running straight in front of him to the horizon – she'd be parked on the side of the road and would flag him down. Provided it wasn't beneath her dignity to do anything so mundane or rational.

Night had fallen properly now and his headlights were the only illumination on the road. Where the hell *was* everybody? He'd been driving less than an hour but he was as alone as if he were on some back road in the middle of the Mojave. And the road itself, and the land around it, didn't seem to jibe with what Jackson knew to be the geography of the area. This straight? This empty? This dark? It was as if he were driving through a vast flat midnight desert bounded to right and left at the limits of his vision by long low hills scarcely distinct in the darkness from the sky above or the ground below.

Paul Simon had just finished assuring him that, though the day was strange and mournful, the mother and child reunion was only a moment away when the radio cut off completely.

No static, no signal fade, just sudden and instant station loss.

He'd have hit the other pre-sets for an alternative had he not realized at that exact moment that the silence was more profound than merely the absence of music. His engine had stopped running too.

"Shit!" he said. His hands flexed instinctively on the wheel. His foot stabbed instinctively in the direction of the brake – but he managed to resist the impulse to slam on and instead tapped at the pedal gently to ease back the momentum that was all that was moving the car.

The lights were still on, thank Christ, so he could guide the car slowly onto the shoulder as it continued to slow. It took about half a minute for it to coast to a perfectly safe stop. Perfectly safe, but come on – the fuck was up with this? Jackson put the car in park and turned the key back to the off position.

Oh man. It was *really* dark without the lights. Jackson felt a sudden stab of unfocussed anxiety and forced himself to take a breath and let his eyes adjust. Alright. That helped. A little.

Through his closed windows, he could hear the chattering of cicadas. He tapped at the plexi-glass of the dash, which was about the extent of his mechanical expertise. None of the dials moved. The car still appeared to have nearly a third of a tank of gas. Already wishing he'd listened when someone had explained to him once how you can tell when you're flooding the engine, he turned the key again.

And again.

Nothing.

The key would click into the first position, powering the lights and electrics, but it simply couldn't make the car start.

He turned it off completely again. It seemed that each time he did, the darkness into which he was plunged was deeper than before but he knew that that was his imagination. He knew that.

He looked out of the windows, ahead and to the sides. Nothing. Alright. Fuck it. What did he pay Triple-A for anyway? He pulled out his cell-phone and powered it up. Reassuring tinkle of chimes .. pretty little screen display .. and then the message *No Service.* He flung it onto the passenger seat to let it keep searching and turned the key one more time.

His headlights stabbed through the night. Directly ahead, caught in the beams like some vaudeville act who'd been standing waiting for their spotlight, were the three sisters.

They were twelve yards or so down the road from his car and appeared to have arrived here with no vehicle of their own. They were wearing matching white gowns and, from this distance, their expressionless faces seemed almost as white against the darkness of the night.

Jackson opened his door and got out, leaving his headlights on. The sweetly overpowering smell of jasmine hit him as, slowly, he walked towards them. He wasn't sure why he didn't call out a greeting. He wasn't entirely sure that a greeting was what he would have called out anyway.

The sisters were silent too, and remained motionless as he approached them.

When he was just a few feet away, the one in the middle – he assumed it was Chinchilla but who could tell? – stepped forward slightly and the ghost of a welcoming smile slid briefly across her lips.

"Mister Jackson," she said. "How lovely to see you again." There was nothing unpleasant about her voice. Not at all. Perhaps just a hint of mild surprise at this converging of paths.

"I was invited," he said. He didn't know why he said that and he didn't like the way his voice sounded saying it, but it didn't seem to bother Chinchilla.

"Oh yes," she said. "You were."

"My car. It's .. stopped. I mean, it won't start."

"That's alright," she said, and her smile grew wider. "You won't be needing it."

She looked as beautiful as ever, but pale. Extremely pale. She leaned a little towards him to say something more and Jackson had to fight the urge to flinch back from her, though there was nothing threatening or fast about her movement and her voice was a delicate and sweet whisper.

"This is the gift we bring you," she said. "The gift of seeing with one's own eyes."

The car's headlights went out.

The moon must have risen while they were talking, or the stars have come out, because Jackson could still see her as she stepped back from him to join her sisters, who moved closer in on either side of her.

There was nothing violent or distressing about the way their flesh melded. It seemed natural and gentle. Like the flow of water into waiting channels or the delicate sweeping application of paint to canvas, the sisters slid into each other effortlessly. Like the sundered images on a stereoscopic photograph marrying themselves to reveal an unsuspected depth, they came together, becoming one.

But not really. Not quite.

There were too many arms. Too many eyes.

The landscape behind seemed to both thicken and recede, losing definition and light, becoming a backdrop, a setting, a black base against which they .. she .. it .. was foregrounded like a surrealist figure on an abstract canvas.

Jackson could still feel the ground beneath his feet. But his other senses were protesting their starvation. The sweet heady smell of the night-blooming jasmine had disappeared and the rhythmic chafing of the cicadas gone with it. His eyes were his only passport to the world and what they saw was already reducing itself to these new essentials. The impossible woman and the darkness behind. That was all there was.

From somewhere within the collage of flesh in front of him, what used to be Chinchilla's mouth smiled again.

And then she was vanishing, all of her was vanishing, shrinking in on herself to a point of dazzling white singularity like the last collapsing sun in a voided universe. Impossibly, piercingly bright. Inconceivably distant. Unutterably beautiful.

And then gone.

There was only the darkness now, a darkness from which all definition and distinction was disappearing.

He was not on the road. He was not in the desert. He was just in the dark. All stars a memory now, and the moon forgotten.

He heard Chinchilla's voice whispering the melody of her Italian song.

And the night peeled open like dark petals.

PRISONERS OF
THE INFERNO

- 1 -

"It's Mickey Rooney," Carducci said, as soon as Jack arrived at his table. "Mickey fucking Rooney. No shit."

The memorabilia dealer's head was twitching in urgent indication and Jack looked back up the length of the convention room in the direction of its spasms.

Flanked on both sides by good-looking young blondes – who, even sitting, had a good five inches on him – Mickey fucking Rooney was indeed seated at one of the autograph tables against the top wall. Jack was surprised that he hadn't noticed him when he came in, but then he tended to ignore the signing tables at these bi-monthly events – usually manned only by second-string TV stars from the 'sixties and 'seventies – and head straight for the regular dealers' tables.

"What's he asking?" Jack said.

"About the same as the kid from *Rin-Tin-Tin*," Carducci said in a can-you-believe-it voice. "Twenty-five if you buy a picture, fifteen for a bring-your-own. You should get something."

Jack shrugged non-committally. "Not my area," he said.

"Not my area," Carducci mimicked. "Get over yourself. He's fucking *golden age*, man! He banged Dorothy, for Christ's sake."

"No, he didn't," Jack said, having no real idea one way or the other.

"Alright, Ava Gardner then. Are you a collector or not?"

"Oh, I'm a collector alright," Jack said. "But apparently not as well-informed a one as I'd thought."

"Yeah?" Carducci said, cocking an interested eyebrow.

Jack lifted his hand to show his friend the item he'd just bought. "How come I haven't heard of this?" he said.

Carducci was an old hand at the poker face but he actually twitched in surprise when he saw what Jack was showing him and, when he reached out to take the front-of-house still for a closer look, he held it almost reverently and was silent for a couple of seconds.

"Where the fuck did you find this?" he said eventually.

Jack had found it while flicking through the four-dollar-per box of eight by tens at some newbie's table. He hadn't expected to come across anything worthwhile and had hardly been paying attention until he'd felt his hands pause.

His practiced fingers, faster than his eye, had frozen in position like they'd just hit a seam of gold in a slate mine and Jack looked down to see what the fuss was about.

The still was sepia-toned rather than simple black-and-white and – judging by the yellowing on the borders and the few tiny cracks here and there in the emulsion – obviously an original. And from at least the mid nineteen-thirties. Maybe even pre-code. Jack lifted it out from among the various worthless dupes of anonymous westerns and forgotten melodramas to look at it more carefully.

The image displayed was of an actress – presumably the lead, though she wasn't anybody Jack recognized – who'd got herself into a bit of bother. She was in the process of being bound to an upright cruciform pillar in some kind of ceremonial chamber – a pretty fucking big one to judge by the hordes of out-of-focus extras in the far background – and was staring in left-of-frame shock at something unseen that was heading her way. Something that meant business, if the look of anticipatory horror on her face was anything to go by.

Her dress had been ripped away from her at both shoulder and thigh but it didn't have the artfully disarranged look you'd expect from a set-dresser's tease. It looked much more urgent than that, looked like something or someone had torn at the cloth in a genuine frenzy to get to the flesh beneath. And the girl's open mouth and wide-eyed mix of expectancy and fear could have given even the great Fay Wray a run for her money.

The image's weirdly erotic charge was undeniable, of course, and was certainly part of what Jack liked about it. But it wasn't just that. It had that *thing*. That thing Jack loved, that sense of what he was being allowed to look at being something other than simply a photograph of a bunch of overpaid people playing dress-up. That was always the secret to the movies he loved. It didn't even have to be in the genre in which he pretended to specialise. It was as deliriously present for him in the art deco dreams of Fred and Ginger as it was when Lon senior strode down the Opera steps in a skull mask and two-strip Technicolor. And this picture had it. In spades. A teasing glimpse from a forgotten world, a world that felt at once utterly real, and yet utterly unreachable.

There was a title running across the border beneath the image. *Prisoners of the Inferno*, it said. Which rang no bells at all, other than the generic. Even then it sounded more like a title from the pulps of the same period than it did a movie. Jack wondered if it might have been a serial rather than a feature, though there was nothing in the rest of the minimal text to suggest that it was.

He took a carefully casual glance at the dealer and at what else was displayed on his table and the wall behind it. He could see in a second that the guy knew nothing. There was a *Topkapi* one-sheet that was way over-priced and a *City of the Dead* lobby card that was hilariously under. Some bandwagon jumper who was pricing his shit by voodoo and what other idiots told him.

Deserved what he got then, didn't he, Jack thought and, surrounding his find on either side with two stills from *Gorgo* (neither featuring the beast), he waved the three of them at the guy as if he was considering doing him the favour of taking this crap off his hands.

"Three for ten?" he asked like it was no biggie, and the money already in his hand like it was a no-brainer.

The dealer looked at the box, looked at Jack, and looked at the cash. Didn't look at the stills. So there went his last chance to say there'd been a mistake. Amateur.

"Okay," he said, prefacing it with a put-upon sigh and treating Jack to a petulant grimace of the you're-killing-me-here variety.

Jack smiled politely, handed over the money, and walked away. The dealer didn't even notice him putting the *Gorgo* pictures back in the box.

❁

Carducci repeated his question, with emphasis.

"Where the *fuck* did you find *this*?" he said.

"In the idiot's come-on box," Jack said, nodding back in the direction of the other guy's table.

Carducci stared across the room with a devastated look of missed opportunity on his face, like it was the day before Prom and he'd just seen the prettiest girl in class say yes to the one guy who'd actually had the balls to ask her.

"Fuck," he said quietly and regretfully.

"So?" Jack said, "What do you know about it?" and Carducci looked back at him.

"You *have* heard of it," he said. "Just not under that name. It was recut and retitled *The Cabinet of Doctor Coppelius* and—"

"Oh, fuck you," Jack said, half disappointed and half-relieved. "You are *so* full of shit. *Coppelius* never existed. It's a ghost film. A hoax."

He remembered the story well. Some buff with a website and too much time on his hands – and, it had to be admitted, more than passing skills at both Photoshop and bullshit – had started a little viral frenzy nearly a decade ago. He'd been smart enough to bury it in an otherwise-accurate filmography rather than write a big splashy piece on the home page. You'd had to be interested enough to be there in the first place (which, for any demographer, pegged you instantly as statistically likely to be an underachieving white male between 25 and 50) and then choose to follow a couple of links. Even when you got there, there was no flashing sign or anything. It was just another item in a fairly exhaustive listing-with-credits of Poverty Row Horrors Yet to be Released on Video. Among the perfectly legitimate and verifiable titles, the webmaster – what was his online name? Cap'n Cadaver? Something equally ludicrous, anyway – had inserted a quiet little entry for a film which nobody'd ever heard of but which the capsule critique made sound like a nasty little treasure.

THE CABINET OF DOCTOR COPPELIUS *US/UK 1932 71 minutes. Dominion Pictures. Alice Lavender, Catherine Hobson, Kurt Crandall, David Batchelor. Dir: Thomas Rheimer, Scr: Patrick Adams, Pr: Carl Bowman, Conrad Fisher.* Less expressionist than the *Caligari* nod in the title might suggest, this low-budget programmer offers instead the kind of unblinking gaze at body-horror that wouldn't become common until after Franju's verité approach many years later. Crandall's mad doctor – hilariously obsessed with Flecker's noted line from *Hassan*, "For lust of knowing what should not be known", which he intones several times with an almost Barrymore level of hammy gravitas – teams with Batchelor's alcoholic toymaker to construct a 'cabinet of transmutation' that transforms several cast-members into life-size dolls who wreak impressively vicious mayhem on several unsuspecting day-players. Lavender, in her only movie, impresses as the plucky gal-reporter swept into the lunacy.

Jack had let himself be drawn in to a couple of message board back-and-forths but the Cap'n – Colonel Carrion, was it? Corporal Carnal? – had stopped posting after several people had called him on his crap and, without a whipping boy to target, the activity on the boards had petered out.

"No," Carducci said to Jack, with the fervency of a true believer – and there'd certainly been some of them, including a handful of hipper-than-thous who claimed to have actually seen a print in revival houses in the 'seventies. "Not a ghost film. A lost film. I mean, *really* lost. Makes *London After Midnight* look like something that gets played every other day on TCM."

Jack took the picture back, pretending not to notice how reluctant Carducci's fingers were to let it go. "Alright," he said. "Even if *that's* true, I never heard this *Prisoners of the Inferno* title mentioned in any of the forums. Why was it re-cut? Why was it re-titled? How do you know it's the same movie?"

"Oh, it *isn't* the same movie," Carducci said. "They cut it a *lot*. The *Coppelius* version never killed anyone."

The website was still there – nothing ever really goes away on the net – but it was pretty damn dormant. The last update, according to the homepage, was a long time ago and the last entry on the forum even older. Jack was more than half-convinced that he was wasting his time when he posted a fairly long open enquiry on the thread about *Coppelius*. He mentioned the original title, even said he'd recently come into possession of an image from the film, but decided not to scan the picture and upload it. For all he knew, he had the last surviving artefact of a truly lost thing and he wasn't going to give it away to bootleggers, even if he doubted that anyone other than him was ever going to visit this site again.

He'd put the still in a Mylar sleeve and perched it in front of his Mr. Coffee so that he could keep looking at it while he nuked himself an excuse for dinner. His computer pinged at him and he wandered from the kitchenette to the main room. He had mail.

The subject-heading was *Prisoners of the Inferno*.

He'd expected no response at all, certainly not this fast and certainly not by e-mail. He'd had to fill out a user profile to post on the site and the e-dress was a required field but, come on, who sends an e-mail instead of just posting on the thread?

The text wasn't as carefully worded as his own, and nowhere near as long-winded.

Very direct in fact. Just six words.

Do you want to see it?

- 2 -

Unlikely to be popcorn then, Jack thought as he pressed the door-bell on the gone-to-shit bungalow in the middle of a tract at the ass-end of Van Nuys.

The door was opened by a woman. She looked about sixty, and like she'd decided not to fight it; muumuu, carpet slippers, can of Molson.

She looked at Jack for less than a second, then turned her head and shouted back into the house. "Walter!"

There was no reply. The woman walked away from the door without saying anything to Jack and he wasn't sure whether to step inside or not. After a moment, a heavyset man in an islands shirt appeared from a door towards the rear of the house. "JRosen101?" he called to Jack without bothering to come to the front door.

Jack nodded. "Jack," he clarified, stepping inside.

"Walter," the guy said. Thirty, maybe older. Hard to tell because the fat of his face kept it wrinkle-free. "Come on." He sounded a little put-out, as if Jack was late or something, keeping people waiting.

The room at the back was tiny but had been set up as a mini theatre with four easy chairs facing a small free-standing screen. Jack was surprised to see an honest-to-God movie projector behind the chairs – he'd expected to be watching a DVD-R at best – but it was too small for 16mm and too ancient for Super-8.

"Standard 8?" Jack asked, kind of delighted.

Walter shook his head as he gestured Jack to take one of the chairs. "Nine point Five," he said.

"You're kidding," Jack said. He'd *heard* of 9.5mm – a home format introduced in the early twenties by Pathé but essentially crushed by Kodak's 8mm just before World War Two – but had never seen either films or hardware. Carducci claimed to have a 9.5 print of Hitchcock's *Blackmail* buried somewhere in his storage space, but then Carducci claimed to have pretty much *everything* buried somewhere.

Another man came into the room. The Stan to Walter's Ollie, he was five-five and rail-thin and sported a pair of black horn-rimmed glasses. Jack wondered if he'd already been in the house, or maybe had a key to the front door.

"Hey, Lenny," Walter said without enthusiasm and glancing at his watch. Jack waited for an introduction that didn't come.

"I'm Jack," he said as Lenny sat down.

"I know," Lenny said. "Did you bring it?"

Jack drew the Mylar-housed still from the computer bag he'd brought – it had been either that or a Trader Joe's tote, nobody had briefcases anymore – and Lenny took a cursory glance at it.

"Very nice," he said and then, half-turning to Walter who was threading up an oversized reel into the projector, "The one Forry had? You think?"

"Probably," Walter said, dimming the lights from a remote.

"Stolen," Lenny said. "He was so *trusting.*"

"Hey," Jack said. "I got this at—"

"No, no, no," Lenny said, interrupting him. "Nobody's accusing *you*. I mean, you *paid* for it, right?"

"Yes, I did," Jack said, refraining from saying how little it had cost him.

"Then it's yours," Lenny said, in an annoyingly kind tone. Like Jack needed *his* fucking blessing.

Walter had sat down. "It's starting," he said, which was Walter for stop talking.

❁

The print was of the later cut, as Walter – he assumed it had been Walter – had told him when he'd replied to Jack's reply and e-mailed him the address. Interestingly, though, the main title card – the one that actually said *The Cabinet of Doctor Coppelius* – was in a font that didn't quite match the cards before and after it, which lent some credence to the idea that the film had once been called something else.

The dupe was a little washed-out – the blacks not really black and the actor's faces occasionally slipping into an unpleasant featurelessness against too bright backgrounds – but was otherwise in remarkably good shape.

The movie itself was worryingly slow-paced, even for Jack – and he was a guy who could sit through the flattest Monogram six-reeler without checking his watch even once – and the acting was as alternately amateurish and histrionic as the website critique had suggested. Jack had begun to worry that, as was depressingly often the case, the mystery and intrigue surrounding a thing's loss was far more entertaining than the found artefact itself but, once he'd let himself relax into the film's wilfully leisurely pacing, he realized he was starting to enjoy it.

The lead girl – Alice Lavender, the girl from his still – helped a lot. She was just adorable as the feisty little heroine trying to impress both her crusty editor and her policeman boyfriend by cracking the story surrounding the mysterious deaths. And the life-size dolls produced from the toymaker's Cabinet and sent forth to murder and mutilate anybody dumb enough to piss off Doctor Coppelius were quite successfully creepy. Their skin, post-transmutation, had a pale inhuman smoothness and there was stitching – rather convincing stitching – on their faces and limbs. Their eyes were completely black – the blackness, unfortunately, put in with a travelling ink-out like they'd given Tom Tyler in one of the *Mummy* sequels – but the fact was that, when the actors stood still long enough for the blobs not to move, the effect was surprisingly powerful.

What was really fascinating – and torturously enticing – was how obvious it actually was that the movie had been cut and had had new scenes added, with both the cuts and the additions serving to dilute whatever power the original may have had. Some of the nastier doll-demon murders simply *stopped* mid-carnage and jump-cut to the next scene, for example, and there was a higher than usual quota of those annoying bits where an Irving the Explainer figure went to quite ridiculous lengths to explain how what might have appeared to be supernatural was actually a combination of engineering wizardry and showmanship gone all evil-genius.

The most egregious and frustrating alteration came at the climax. The movie built to the capture of Alice's character by Coppelius and his toymaker and her insertion into the Cabinet. Thrillingly, unlike every other transformation, the camera followed her in. The Cabinet was bigger on the inside. Much bigger. So much so that it soon became clear that the inside of the Cabinet wasn't the inside of the Cabinet at all. The Cabinet was a portal to Hell and its unlucky entrants were quite literally prisoners of the inferno. This was where Jack's still had come from, this sequence in which the fetishized binding of the girl took on an overwhelming and shaming erotic power. And then – just as she was being dragged from the pillar toward the disturbingly elaborate doll-making machinery – another of those obvious cuts happened and the whole sequence was revealed as being merely the nightmare of the kidnapped girl *before* she was put into the Cabinet. And then, of course, the door burst open and her policeman boyfriend rescued her.

Jack *knew* that it hadn't been a dream in the original and that *Prisoners of the Inferno* must have culminated not only in the activation and operation of the machinery but in the re-opening of the Cabinet and the disgorging of whatever doll-demon Alice had been turned into. He ached to see it.

❀

It was starting to rain when they came out and Jack found himself standing on the kerb next to Lenny, both of them looking up at the sky with the vaguely hard-done-to expression common to non-native Angelenos whenever the weather wasn't perfect. As if Southern California had misled them, brought them here under false pretences, strung them along like a lover who waits till after the wedding to mention that occasional little problem with bipolar disorder.

Lenny caught Jack's eye. "Did you like it?" he asked.

"Yeah," Jack said. "I did. Overall. How about you?"

"Not as good as the real thing," Lenny said, almost distractedly, as he pulled his jacket over his head like a makeshift hoodie and ran for his car.

- 3 -

Carducci had a small store in one of the commercial alleys off Hollywood Boulevard. Some nice stuff, but mainly repros and shit for the tourists. Kept the prime material for the conventions and the auctions.

"Oh, right," he said, when Jack swung by to ask him about Walter. "Fat guy, Hawaiian shirts? Lives with his mother in some piss-poor shack the top of Van Nuys?"

Jack deadpanned him. "Didn't you just describe every one of your customers?" he said. Couldn't help it.

"Oh really?" Carducci said, looking Jack up and down blankly, like the sneer was implicit. "Who died and made you Johnny fucking Depp?"

Jack grinned, letting it go. "What about his friend Lenny?" he said. "Little guy? Horn-rims?"

"*He* was there?"

"Yeah. Like he had bragging rights. Thought he might have been, you know, the boyfriend or something."

"Stay the fuck away from *that* guy," Carducci said. "Seriously. Grade-A creep."

"What? Like a prick?"

"No. Like a fucking *creep*. As in creeps-me-out. For real. Him and his whole nasty little crowd. Used to hang around with Kenny Anger and LaVey. Seriously. They're not into this stuff for the same reasons we are. Got their own agenda. Not nice people."

Carducci's reads on people were usually pretty good so when Jack got the phone-call from Lenny a couple of days later he wanted to be guarded and careful. But he couldn't be, not when he knew that Lenny – creep or not – could have only one reason for calling, that he was going to offer access to a print of the real thing, to *Prisoners of the Inferno*. He wondered if this was how newly-hooked junkies felt when they got the first follow-up call from their dealer. Because that's what he was, Jack realised. Hooked. Hooked from the moment he'd stared at the still for the first time and felt that intoxicating rush of being allowed to gaze at the forbidden.

He had no doubt that it was going to cost him this time. Wasn't that how it always worked with junkies and their dealers? But he didn't care. He'd empty his fucking savings account if that's what they asked. He wanted to see more. He wanted to see, he wanted to know. *For lust of knowing what should not be known*, he thought, remembering Doctor Coppelius's knee-jerk little mantra.

But Lenny didn't mention money at all.

"You seemed . . . *intrigued*," he said, as if that were perhaps payment enough.

"Well, yeah," Jack said. Because he, you know, *was*. The fuck else was he going to say?

Lenny didn't reply. Like he was waiting for Jack to ask, and enjoying the wait.

"You said, *not as good as the real thing*," Jack said eventually, but still got nothing in return. "The other night." Just the sound of Lenny breathing. "In the rain." He didn't know why the fuck he mentioned the rain.

"I'm going to give you an address, Jack," Lenny finally said. "It's a private address, and I don't want you to write it down. Is that alright?"

Jack said that yeah that was alright and Lenny gave him the address and Jack repeated it and Lenny said he'd see him in half an hour and hung up.

It only took twenty minutes – no traffic for a change – and Jack circled the block a few times so as not to look too eager. It was a shitty apartment building on Franklin, one of those four boxes on top of four more with railed walkways running past all the front doors like the place had wanted to be a motel but had been too stoned to build a fucking lobby.

Jack rapped his knuckles on the third door of the upper level because the bell didn't work – *quelle surprise* – and Lenny opened it and ushered him inside. An old man sat in a La-Z-Boy with a blanket over his legs and smiled at Jack with a vague delight, like he couldn't ever remember anymore if he'd met someone previously but had learned to err on the side of presuming he had. *Really* old. Like he'd cracked a century or was about to.

"Hey there," said Jack, returning the smile. And that seemed to be it for the socializing because Lenny already had his fingers on the handle of the door to the apartment's only other room. "In here," he said, waiting till Jack was practically bumping into the door before pushing it gently open and stepping back to let Jack enter.

Lenny didn't follow him in. "We'll give you some privacy," he said and, even as he was closing the door, Jack saw him half-turn towards the old man. "Shall I make you a pot of tea, David?" he said, just before the door clicked shut.

The room wasn't dark at all, though the light from the three grime-encrusted bulbs in the ceiling housing was a dull and bilious yellow. It had been intended as a bedroom, Jack assumed, but it now served another purpose and was untroubled by either furniture or people.

It wasn't empty, though.

There was no projector this time, because no projector was needed. Jack hadn't been brought here to see a film. Lenny hadn't been talking about a print, uncut or otherwise. When he'd said they had the real thing, he meant the real thing.

He meant the Cabinet.

It stood in the centre of the room, looking surprisingly substantial for something that was supposed to have been built over seventy-five years ago for a low-budget movie. Good condition, too, with only some rust-stains here and there on its patterned brass filigree to show the passage of time.

If Lenny locked the door to the room from the other side Jack couldn't hear it. Not above the waltz-time minor-key melody that began to sound from somewhere inside the Cabinet, mechanical and painful, like it was escaping a music-box built from razors and bone.

The Cabinet door creaked slowly open.

And Alice Lavender stepped out.

She was beautiful still, unchanged from what those audiences must have seen nearly eighty years ago. Unchanged by age, at least. But the Cabinet had done its work and her transmutation was long complete.

The doll girl, pale stitched face expressionless, black marble eyes glinting only with reflected light, came towards Jack with a mechanised grace, her head tick-tocking rhythmically from side to side and her slender limbs clicking audibly with each automaton step.

The fingers of her left hand ratcheted open one by one as she extended her hand to Jack.

Not in threat.

In dreadful invitation.

The transition from the initial darkness of the Cabinet's interior to the infernal light glowing endlessly from vast and distant furnaces was seamless. Jack was one place, and then he was another.

He couldn't tell when Alice had let go of his hand.

"Welcome," said the Doctor, as he turned his own hands to show Jack his palms and the terrible implements that bloomed from their stigmata. "Time to play."

THE GIRL IN
THE BLUE VOLCANO

Yeah, yeah. Don't get all excited. It's just a bar. *The Blue Volcano*. Buried in the middle of a strip mall at the corner of Pico and who gives a shit.

I know. You'd think a bar stuck with a location like that – because, trust me, Iowa, it's not an area where you're going to see Young Hollywood out bar-hopping, not even on a bet – would know its place, call itself something bland and honest like *Joey's* or *Mikey's*. You know, keep its fucking head down. But no. It had to aspire. Adorable. Or pathetic. Depends on which of your medications was kicking in at the time.

Something else – I promise I'll get off this in a minute – You'd figure, wouldn't you, that if they were going to go all showboaty on the name front like that then they must've put some thought into it, figure that what they were going for, what they wanted to imply, was some retro-hip conceptual collision. You know; Blue – the color of after-hours jazz, the color of cool; and Volcano – eruptive, happening, hot. Yeah, well save it for your book report, kids. The naming was depressingly literal. There was a large painting hanging behind the bar – and when I say painting, I'm being very kind to the Special Needs genius who shot his wad on the canvas – and guess what it was a painting of?

Nice. Collect your steak knives, and thanks for being on the show.

Now, you *could* – I mean, provided you were less prone to ADD than me and the rest of the 21st fucking century – spend hours wondering about the circumstance that would force any self-respecting bar-owner to put something that spectacularly bloody awful in plain sight of patrons from whom he expected to take money – lost a bet; pissed somebody off; blind – but my buddy Occam's got a real sharp razor that says this particular bar-owner simply *liked* the piece of shit. Must have. Guy'd even had a little brass plaque made that sat on the bottom edge of the frame and told you the title of the picture in the kind of fancy curled lettering that was all the rage back when people could still do joined-up writing.

The Girl in the Blue Volcano, it said.

Which was all fine and good, but there was no girl in the picture.

Jill Gillespie had told me about the place a couple of nights before. Apart from everything else, she knew I always liked a quiet little nook to have a drink and she'd not been kidding about this one's crowd-free ambience. Apart from the hired hand behind the bar – silent and expressionless, big enough to double as a bouncer, wiping and re-wiping unused glasses slowly and constantly like he'd listed OCD in the special skills box on his application form – I was the only one in there. I was on my second Vodka straight – fuck your lime-juice, who're you trying to kid? – when some slow piano chords drifted out from the jukebox, stately and melancholy. Jackson Browne. *For a Dancer.* I couldn't help it. I smiled.

Yeah, yeah. I know. Seventies soft-rock, staggeringly unhip, couldn't be less cool if you put a fucking match to it, but I like it. So sue me. Roll over Moby and tell Miley Cyrus the news. Besides, what was interesting was that I'd lay good money there wasn't another jukebox within a hundred square miles that would have had that song on it and I'd double down against anybody actually selecting it.

"Well, well, well," a voice from the old country said behind me. "Look who it isn't."

Look who it isn't. Jesus Christ. I don't think anybody'd said that since David Bowie sent his last spandex to Goodwill. I wouldn't have bothered turning around, except that I knew the voice and I understood completely why the song was on his jukebox. He'd always liked it. It let him pretend he had a soul.

Spider Ballantyne. Stephen to his friends. I'd never heard anybody call him Stephen. Little older. Little balder. Ugly as ever.

"Kitty fucking Donnelly," he said, with that ridiculous mix of affection and contempt upon which his particular class of Irish dickhead has prided itself since the first apples grew on the grave of Cuchulainn. "Let me look at you."

Yeah, like he'd wait for permission. His watery eyes roved me up and down with an instinctive professional appraisal – he'd once run a stable of little green-eyed hookers in Hell's Kitchen, most of them straight off the Belfast boat – and gave me an approving nod.

"Easiest money in the world, young Kathleen," he said automatically.

I let it go. It was just pavlovian with the guy. "This is *your* place, Spider?" I said.

"Oh, now don't you be teasing me, Kitty," he said. "You didn't know? You're telling me you didn't get all dressed up like that specially to come and see old Spider?"

Dressed up. Halter top, jeans, and Chuck Taylor's. Asshole.

"I had no idea," I said, shaking my head. "Just wanted a drink."

"Really? No idea that your old friend Spider was now a respectable publican. Just happened to be passing."

"Had a little business to take care of in the neighbourhood," I said.

"I'll not ask," he said, and winked. "Different line these days, I gather. Not running the candy for Paulie Benson anymore."

"Paulie met with an accident," I said.

"So I heard," he said, and looked at me some more.

He planted himself on the stool next to mine and waved a lazy finger to catch his barkeep's attention. "Ms. Donnelly's money is no good here," he said. There might have been a nod from the guy in response, but the machine's not been made that could've measured it.

Spider decided that he wasn't yet done with the auld lang syne hospitality. He swung on the stool to actually look at the barman. "In fact, let's shut it down," he said. "Closed for a private party. The punters will just have to look elsewhere tonight for their cup of welcome."

Well, that was obviously going to break a thousand eager hearts in the neighbourhood. I'd have assumed Spider was joking, but positive thinking had always been his mantra and irony never his strong suit. The barkeep hit a couple of switches behind the bar and the spill of neon from the *Blue Volcano* sign outside disappeared, along with the two overheads that had thrown their dim yellow glow over the handful of tables between the bar and the paint-blackened plate-glass window. I thought I heard a small click too, as if a latch might have locked into place on the door. Yeah, I know. But it doesn't mean they're not after you.

There were a couple of mood lights glinting through the towered and racked bottles of Jameson's and shit, but the main light now came from the gallery-style tracks tilted down to bathe the painting. Thorough job, and nice effect. Really brought the thing to life, like the light was shining out from within rather than the other way around. Still looked like it was painted by Rainman after a fine meal of the wrong kind of mushrooms, but you could certainly see it better now, rich blue bouncing off it and giving the whole room a kind of underwater vibe.

Spider nodded at the painting without actually looking in its direction. "Nice, eh?" he prompted, with a certain pride in ownership.

I gave him a slow grin. It wasn't overly rich in ambiguity, but he chose to rise above the contempt.

"Came to me as part of a complicated settlement," he said, as if he thought I might actually be interested. I wasn't surprised to hear that. Most of Spider's settlements were complicated.

I looked at the picture again, seemed rude not to, and was unprepared for how much it wanted to hold my attention. When I looked back at Spider, he seemed surprised that I had.

"Something troubling you, Kitty?" he said.

"I don't see the girl," I said to him.

"Well, you wouldn't, would you?" he said. "I mean, the picture's not called *The Girl* on *the Blue Volcano*, now is it?" He looked over my shoulder to wink at the guy wiping the glasses. Like they were both in on a gag that was probably over the head of a silly little thing like me.

Turning back to give me the benefit of his full attention, Spider turned on the charm. He certainly had the blarney down, I'll give him that, silver tongue caressing his words and sending them my way like flowers and kisses from some bastard child of W. B. Yeats and the gentlest of sugar-daddy seducers. We chatted away for a good five minutes, covering the latest news on mutual acquaintances from the old neighbourhood back east and the problems facing any poor young girl making her way in the modern world. He was solicitous and attentive, his eyes flicking only occasionally to my glass and to the unlabelled decanter from which it had been filled.

My eyes were drawn increasingly to the painting behind the bar. Spider might have glanced at it once or twice during our little chat but if he had he'd been subtle enough about it that I hadn't realized just how much he was controlling my attention and directing my gaze. He'd always been good at that, at the unstated suggestion, always been good at manoeuvring little girls into places and positions of his choosing without making them notice the manipulation until they were giving it up for cents on the dollar and all their pretty dreams were dust and memory.

But Spider wasn't saying anything now. Nothing that I could make sense of anyway. He was still letting the words pour forth, but they'd ceased to matter as words, at least to me. Staring at the picture, strangely unwilling to look away, I could only hear them as sounds, like they were just nonsense syllables strung upon the haunting melody that seemed to be the secret theme and eternal pulse of the place I was being allowed to see. There was so much more in the painting than I'd first noticed, so much detail and depth. The runnels on the side of the volcano were deep and forested, giving a sense of scale to the whole environment that was dizzying. There were blue stone cities hiding within those valleys, long abandoned and left to the shadowed things which had inherited them. And there were cracks in the valley floors, cracks in the world, giving on to the lakes of fire within. I'd known that the sky was the wrong color back when I was standing on the slopes, but the sky was far behind me now and there were only the red stone roofs miles above the seething pools. It wasn't like falling, it was like floating, like flying, and as the lakes rippled into open wounds, as the vast creatures that dwelt within them rose in hungry welcome, I knew that . . .

Fuck knows how I managed to raise my hand, but I slashed a fingernail across my lower lip and drew blood and the beautiful searing pain threw me back, rocking, on my stool.

A sound escaped Spider's mouth, somewhere between a sigh of frustration and a hiss of anger. I couldn't look at him yet, kept my eyes locked on the edge of the bar, clinging to the solidity of its cigarette scars and glass stains like anchors in a loosened world. I could hear my heart pounding arhythmically like it was struggling to recover from the killing rush of an amyl overdose.

"Oh, Kitty, Kitty, Kitty," Spider said, like a hurt but patient Prom date I'd just stopped at second base. "You were so close, my darling. So close. There's no point to this fighting, you know. Not now. Surrender is going to make it so much easier for you. Swear to God"

I could feel him watching me try to shake my head, as if I needed to clear it. It was difficult. "Spider," I said. "What . . . what the fuck *is* this? What the hell have you gotten yourself involved with?"

I forced myself to look over at him. He gave me a searching look before he spoke, letting himself be sure that I was way past the point at which he needed to pretend anymore. "Oh now, Kitty," he said. "The truth is I wasn't as completely honest with you as I perhaps should have been. You have to see that a man born to a trade is naturally reluctant to change it, even when forced by dint of circumstance into new business partnerships. Old dog. New tricks. You understand."

I was beginning to. His trade mightn't have changed, but I was pretty fucking sure his clientele had.

"It'll not be much longer now, sweetheart," he said. His voice was melodious and comforting and he stroked gently at the hand I'd put on the bar to steady myself. "Take another little look at the picture, why don't you?" He gave it a moment. "No? Not yet? Well, that's alright, my darling. That's perfectly alright. Stephen Ballantyne has never rushed a lady in his life."

He turned to the barman. "Why don't you give Ms. Donnelly another shot?" he said. "For old times' sake, Kitty," he added, turning to me as the guy dutifully topped up my glass.

I managed to calm my breath. The world seemed solid again, solid as it ever would. I found my voice enough to not let him hear it tremble.

"For a dancer," I said, raising the glass in a tiny salute in his direction.

"That's the girl," he said, with loving parental approval. He didn't make a big deal out of me not actually sipping any of it yet. He noticed. But he and his clients were patient, and the night was young.

His mistake was thinking that I was already two glasses in.

Like I said, Spider's pretty good at that whole don't let the other person see what you're doing routine. But I'm not too fucking shabby at it either. And I was fairly sure that the sticky little pool of doctored vodka at the foot of my stool wasn't going to be the worst stain Spider's cleaning service had ever had to deal with.

"You know, Spider," I said. "Truth is, I wasn't completely honest with *you*, either. I *did* know that this was your bar. I had a chat with Jill Gillespie the other night."

"Jill Gillespie . . ." he said, like somebody making an honest effort to remember. "Remind me?" He was waving one hand in the air as if to pluck the elusive memory from the ether, first two fingers semi-upright like he was the fucking Pope or something.

"Jesus Christ, Spider," I said. "You don't even remember their *names*, now?"

He gave the little grin that he thought passed for contrite while his eyes twinkled with the ersatz charm that had always won him indulgent forgiveness from the harshest of critics.

Not this time.

"You probably got her talking," I said. "You always do. Let her story fall over you, let her think you were listening while you were already doping her up and planning the delivery. She was a dancer, if that rings any bells." I nodded at the silent jukebox. "You probably played the Jackson Browne for her to help close the deal."

I saw the memory seat itself in his eyes, followed very quickly by a look of confusion. No, that's not right. A look like he thought *I* was confused. "If it's the young lady I'm thinking of," he said, his voice becoming just a tad more careful and considered, "I think it's . . . unlikely . . . that you've spoken to her since I last saw her."

"Yeah?" I said. "That what you think?"

Jill had simply shown up.

I'd been in the middle of a DVR marathon of *Gilmore Girls* – what, you wanna make something of it? – and one second I'd been alone and the next I hadn't. None of your bullshit chain rattling or window tapping first, none of your frost forming on the counterpane or cold spots hovering in the air. Just Jill, there, next to the bed, her face looking nothing like crumpled linen and her body looking just like her body. Apart from the, you know, spectral glow and occasional transparency.

She had no idea how long she had to talk – yeah, like I *did* – so she told her story with a clarity and economy that had really never been in her nature. But then her nature was something she was in the process of shedding.

She didn't weep. She wasn't angry.

I did. I was.

"She looked good," I said. "Wanted to be remembered to you."

Spider was staring at me, like he was wondering if this little story of mine was some heretofore unexpected side-effect of the drugs he hid in his drinks.

"You're not the only one who's changed trades, Spider," I said. "Paulie was my last boss. I don't have employers anymore, I have clients. I'm a private operative."

He must have noticed by now that I wasn't so fucking woozy as I'd let him believe, but his chuckle still had a practiced and confident condescension. "You always did have an inflated opinion of yourself, young Kitty," he said. "I should have taken you to task years ago." His lip curled into a sneer. "*Private operative.* Fuck you. Far as I'm concerned, you're nothing. Nothing but a sad little dyke with ideas above her station."

"No, Spider," I said and, just for a moment, just for shits and giggles, I let my precious disaffect slip from my voice. "As far as you're concerned, I am the Red Right Hand. I'm the angel of fucking death."

He heard me. His head jerked toward the barman again, ready to give him the high-sign. But I spoke to the guy first.

"2719 Rossmore, isn't it?" I said.

The barman didn't say anything but, if they hadn't killed the lights earlier, I think we'd have seen him grow a little paler. I tossed him my cell. "You're on speed-dial," I said. "Three."

I couldn't hear what his daughter said to him, but I think she must have remembered most of what I'd told her. And, besides, how many ways are there for an eight-year-old to say *Daddy, there's a big black motherfucker with a knife at my throat*?

"You remember Micky Gundry, don't you, Spider?" I said. "You always used to make that stupid joke, *Now that's what I call Black Irish*. Micky's always up for a job. I couldn't meet his usual price, of course. But you know me. A right little charmer when I need something done fast. And besides, he fucking *hates* you."

The barman put the phone down on the bar and looked at Spider. "I'm sorry, Mr. Ballantyne," he said, and got the hell out of Dodge.

First words he'd spoken all night, and enough of the trace of the brogue in there to piss me off and almost regret not making him stay for the party after all. I am *so* over these Old Country assholes. It's always something with them. No frigging downtime at all. Not if there's some poor sucker to be screwed over. Ripping you off on the bar tab, forgetting they borrowed your DVDs, throwing virgins – or an item of similar value – into extra-dimensional volcanoes. It never ends. Sometimes you take the time to outwit them. Sometimes you just stab them in the fucking face.

Spider was stupid enough to turn and watch his bartender leave. Like he thought I was going to wait for a referee to read us the rules? The sound of the glass smashing against the brass rail snapped his head back in my direction, just in time for him to see the sharp and shattered rim heading his way before it drove itself deep into his cheek.

I cleared up a little and re-locked the doors. I had everything ready in a couple of minutes. Burning the painting was no problem. You didn't have to look at an alcohol-sprayed canvas to toss a match in its general direction.

I put his favourite song back on the jukebox, partly because it seemed appropriate and partly because it's just so fucking beautiful. Gentle and wise and measured and hopeful, it's a song about how death comes for us all, but how it's our duty to live well and kindly, about how we learn from seeds scattered by others and how we should go ahead and scatter some seeds of our own, about how there may be reasons we were alive that we'll never know.

Jackson Browne is so much nicer than me.

Because I knew why *I* was alive, at least for the next ten minutes.

There was a pickle jar on the bar. I fished out the tiny two-pronged fork and walked over to where I'd strapped Spider to his pool table.

The eight ball in his mouth prevented him from saying anything but the panic in his eyes was eloquent enough. Spider knew what was coming. He knew me, though he'd fooled himself into forgetting. I had a pool cue, a pickle fork, and an active imagination.

Spider was frightened.

Spider was fucked.

I let him look at me for quite some time before I began. He'd always liked looking at pretty young things.

"For a dancer," I said, and made the first incision.

THE SHOW MUST GO ON

DEPARTMENT OF RECONSTRUCTION
INTER-OFFICE MEMO # 249
RE: YOURS OF THURSDAY
Attached please find an E-mail chain recovered from Server#117 (Los Angeles/San Fernando Valley). Chain re-ordered to oldest first for convenience. Please advise re: deletion.

Sent from: upstartcrow117@aol.com
To: ScottC@NewRidgeEntertainment.com
Sent: Wednesday, June 19th 3:27 PM
Subject: Already Rollin'!

Hey Scott,

Excellent meeting yesterday! Too bad Larry couldn't be there himself, but I understand. And it was great to meet with you and Craig anyway. Exciting ideas! I love the way you guys are always thinking ahead of the curve.

So listen: I was really jazzed by some of the shit we were throwing around and - couldn't help it - I hit the keys the second I got back.

Now we both know that my agent would kill me if I went ahead and attached any actual *pages* before we have an actual *deal*, so please regard the stuff pasted in below as just thoughts. Random thoughts. Really specific random thoughts. Really specific, sequenced, structured random thoughts. The sort of sequenced and structured random thoughts that a casual observer might understandably mistake for, you know, the opening seven pages of a screenplay or something. But which absolutely aren't the opening seven pages of a screenplay. Not At All. Because that would be wrong. ;-)

                    ZOMBIE BITCH GOT GAME
                      Not a Screenplay
                            By
                      Cliff Brightwell

        FADE IN:

        EXTEME CLOSE UP: An EYE staring out at us.

        Wide open. Unblinking.

        Is there a thought there? An emotion? Maybe
        fear? We don't have time to guess. Because,
        suddenly ...

        ... the eye EXPLODES outwards in a viscous
        shower of blood and membrane. Right at us. Right
        at us. Like if it was 3-D, we'd be trying to
        wipe the cum-like gunk off our horrified faces.

        Chasing the blood'n'slime out of the cavity of

116

the socket comes the tip of the nine-inch
RAILROAD SPIKE that did it.

CUT TO WIDE to reveal that the eye had belonged
to a ZOMBIE - some undead motherfucker all
gray-pallor, open-wounds, and rotting clothes
- who's now twitching galvanically like a freshly-
zapped steer in a slaughterhouse.

The railroad spike twists professionally in the
eye-cavity like it's making a clean bore and
- after a couple more nauseating seconds of its
spastic death-dance - the Zombie collapses,
revealing behind it...

JACK STUYVESANT - 26, handsome, cool, totally
ripped - who pulls the spike from out the back
of the Zombie's head and wipes it clean on his
wife-beater.

He looks across to the girl who he's just saved
from being the Zombie's lunch.

This is CLAIRE GALLIGAN. Claire's our leading
lady, which means - in case you've been too
busy splitting the atom or curing cancer to
have watched any movies in the last fifty fucking
years - that she's 21 and hot. No, I mean really
hot. Megan Fox hot.

                    JACK
          You all done shopping?

Claire looks around at the derelict CLOTHING
STORE in which they're standing.

                    CLAIRE
          Red is so last year.

The store is a BLOODBATH. Gallons of blood paint
the walls and floor, some of it dried and rusting,
most of it new and running.

Despite its abattoir-chic overlay, the store is
still full of whatever was in style the week
the world ended.

It's also full of CORPSES. They're everywhere,
some human, some zombies.

A free-standing CLOTHES RACK is immediately
behind Claire. Twenty ZOMBIES dangle from it,
hooks through their skulls. Most of them have
gone where the good Zombies go, but two or
three are still twitching.

Without batting an eyelid, Claire pushes two
twitching Zombies apart on the rack to get at
a tiny TUBE-TOP between them.

                    CLAIRE
          But this is cute.

Slipping the tube-top from its hanger, Claire
peels off her blood-and-gore-soaked T-shirt.

Though every guy in the theatre has just decided
he's had more than his ticket-money's worth,
there's no reaction from Jack as he watches
Claire change tops. Because he's, you know,
cool.

Claire wriggles into the tight-fitting top. As she smoothes the fabric over her belly, leaving enough midriff eye-candy to keep the rest of us happy, she looks up at Jack.

                    CLAIRE
          That's better.
                    (beat)
          Duck.

Claire grabs up her hip-mounted SPIKE-LAUNCHER – a kind of zipgun-on-steroids fitted with an oversized revolver-style cylinder loaded with ten Spikes – and fires one directly at Jack ...

... who drops instantly into a crouch ...

... as the spike slams unerringly into the forehead of a FAT FEMALE ZOMBIE whose blubbery arms were about to grab Jack from behind.

As the Zombie hits the ground, quivering into death, Claire cocks her head and gives it a quizzical look.

                    CLAIRE
          Right. Like they have <u>your</u> size in
          stock.

Jack straightens up and nods at Claire.

                    JACK
          Thanks. Where the hell d'ya think
          <u>she</u> came from?

                        CLAIRE
                  (looking past Jack)
            Probably the same place they did.

Jack spins around to see that, at the back of
the store, a set of double FIRE DOORS have been
slammed open ...

... and countless ZOMBIES are pouring in like
bargain hunters on a day-after-thanksgiving
sale. And Jack and Claire appear to be this
year's tickle-me-fucking-Elmo.

Claire glances down at her Spike-Launcher.
Suddenly its nine remaining Spikes seem woefully
inadequate. She looks up to meet Jack's eyes.

                         JACK
            Don't worry, I called us a cab.

BAM!! The entire side wall of the store explodes
as a CLASSIC BLACK LONDON TAXI smashes through
it, hurtles forward twenty feet, and screeches
to a halt right in front of Jack and Claire.

The cab's window cranks down and the driver
leans out. Meet KEVIN. Your classic sidekick.
A just past college-age overweight schlub. Over-
educated. Under-achieving. Way too fond of STAR
TREK. Never been laid.

[Scott - is Jonah Hill too expensive?]

Kevin looks at Jack and Claire and then at the
scores of Zombies heading their way. He calls
out to Jack in a mockney-accent that is every

bit as bad as your classic MARY POPPINS Dick
Van Dyke.

                    KEVIN
        Gor Bloimey, Guv'nor. This better be
        a bloomin' big tip.

Kevin brings his arms up out the driver's window.
Each one holds a double-barreled Spike-firing
CROSSBOW.

As Jack and Claire clamber hurriedly into the
back of the taxi, Kevin takes out the first four
Zombies with a skill and accuracy that almost
lift him out of nerd status.

As he reloads the crossbows from a QUIVER of
Spikes dangling from the rear-view, he shouts
over his shoulder.

                    KEVIN
        You in?

                    JACK
            (slamming passenger door)
        Just drive!

                    KEVIN
        Stone the bleedin' crows, mate. No
        need to get stroppy.

THWACK!!! Taking out another four zombies, Kevin
floors it in reverse and does a stunning rubber-
burning one-eighty to face the front of the
store ...

... and the taxi stalls.

The remaining Zombies race to close the distance, undead arms scrabbling at the back of the cab, rotting mouths chomping in anticipation.

                    CLAIRE
        Fuck!

                    KEVIN
        Ooh-er, missus. And there was me
        finkin' you was a proper lidy.

                    JACK
        Move!
                (beat)
        And drop the accent.

                    KEVIN
                (plain American)
        Geez, Jack. Just tryin' to give you
        some local color.

SLAM! A Zombie has clambered onto the trunk of the cab and is flailing at the rear window.

As the zombie's putrescent face presses hungrily against the glass ...

... Jack snatches Claire's Launcher and, pressing it tight against the window, blasts a spike right through it and directly into the Zombie's forehead.

The taxi's engine stutters back into life.

                    KEVIN
                (chatty, informational)
        Hey, did you know these things run on Diesel?

                    CLAIRE
              (shut the fuck up)
        Kevin!!

Kevin revs it and the Taxi jets forward, clambering
Zombies flung from its trunk as it races toward
the store's big PLATE GLASS WINDOW ...

                    KEVIN
            (calmly professional)
        Please buckle up for safety and comfort.

CUT TO:

EXT. HARRODS, PICCADILLY CIRCUS - SUNSET

The front of Harrods, London's famous department
store.

We get about half a second to take in its olde
worlde splendor ...

... and then its main front window explodes as
Kevin's Taxi comes flying through the air to
land in the middle of Piccadilly Circus.

At the far side of the Circus is LONDON BRIDGE,
its famous towers bathed in the setting sun.
SHAMBLING SHAPES are silhouetted as they shuffle
their way over the Thames river. The Circus is
totally overrun by marauding Zombies. Hundreds
of them. The various London THEATRES are derelict,
their neon signs long-dead and their posters
peeling. Even the famous CAVERN CLUB, home of
the Beatles, is a lightless hulk.
But it's ST PAUL'S CATHEDRAL that seems to be

ground zero for the hordes of the undead. Beneath its famous dome, its doors are open and spilling thousands of Zombies into the Circus.

The landing of Kevin's taxi hasn't exactly gone unnoticed. Every zombie starts shambling towards it.

> KEVIN
> I hate fucking Zombies.

> CLAIRE
> Then stop fucking them.

> KEVIN
> Easy for you to say. You can get dates.

> JACK
> Give me a crossbow.

Jack hands her launcher back to Claire as Kevin tosses him one of the crossbows.

> JACK
> Let's go.

Claire and Jack lower their windows and start firing at the Zombies as Kevin starts the Taxi up.

> KEVIN
> Little road music?

He punches the cab's radio into life as he accelerates. Some long-dead Glam Rocker starts warbling instructions to ride a white swan like the people of the Beltane as the taxi plows forward mercilessly, zombies falling beneath its eager wheels like so much undead road-kill.

As the cab sweeps past the doors of the cathedral, the spewing ranks of Zombies pause and part, to reveal a single figure standing on the steps.

Their leader.

He's all dolled up in moldering MADNESS OF KING GEORGE drag - you know, britches and silk, doublet and hose and shit - and his long ringleted WIG looks particularly bizarre over his pockmarked cadaverous face.

There's something odd about that face. No, I mean odder than the standard-issue undead look.

It's the eyes.

Unlike the glazed and cretinous hungry-and-nothing-more expression shared by every other back from the grave shambler, this fucker's eyes gleam with a kind of malevolent intelligence. Like it knows what it's doing, and likes it.

This is NICHOLAS HAWKSWORTH. Master Architect. Black Magician. King Zombie.

[Hey Scott, it is "Hawksworth", right? That church-builder guy you mentioned? Google's down again, and I'm fucked if I'm driving to the library to check this shit right now. Once you *pay* me, I'll do my research ;-). Anyway, where were we . . .]

Hawksworth points dramatically across the distance at the cab and stares, his eyes locked on Jack and Claire and tracking them as they move. His mouth opens - revealing a strange SWARMING BLACKNESS within it - and a wordless ROAR of challenge echoes over the Circus.

At the eerie sound of their master's voice, the other Zombies fling themselves with renewed rage at the Taxi, as if intending to stop it by sheer weight of numbers.

Claire, grabbing something out of her purse, leans out the window and meets the Hawksworth-thing's eyes, an I'm-so-over-your-bullshit look on her drop-dead face.

Her thumb is poised elegantly at the top of her lipstick ...

                    CLAIRE
          Eat me.

Claire depresses her thumb.

Not a lipstick.

A detonator.

BOOOOOOOOOOOMMM!!!!!!!!!!

The BIGGEST FUCKING EXPLOSION you've ever seen in your entire movie-going life. Suck on it, Michael Bay. Kiss my white ass, Roland Emmerich. Go eat at the kids' table, JJ Abrams.
The Cathedral - fuck it, the whole of Piccadilly

Circus - ignites into a FIRESTORM that makes Dresden look like a sparkler and Nagasaki like a roman candle.

As the flames entirely fill the frame, DEBRIS comes hurtling toward us: Bricks, mortar, body-parts ...

... culminating in Hawksworth's severed head spinning right at us.

Just as the head "reaches" us, its eyes flick open and its undead mouth opens in a silent SCREAM ...

... and the head EXPLODES into a TSUNAMI OF PLAGUE FLEAS. Hundreds of the little bastards. Thousands. Fucking millions. Writhing, twitching, jumping, biting ...

SMASH TO BLACK and crank up the Metallica Cue.

RUN OPENING TITLES

There it is.
Whaddaya think?
You wet? Cause I'm hard.
Let's *do* this mofo, beyotch!

Cheers,

Cliff

P.S. Don't crap your pants that I've killed off our lead villain in the pre-creds. What I'm figuring is that the surviving now-we're-*really*-pissed Zombies find the reconstituted head, skewer it on a stick for safe-keeping, and later insert it into another zombie body which is then animated by Hawksworth's undead intelligence. New body doesn't even have to be a human one. Who says this plague is limited to homo sapiens? Zombie wolf body. Zombie gorilla body. Whatever we want. Cool? Damn straight.

Sent from: ScottC@NewRidgeEntertainment.com
To: upstartcrow117@aol.com
Sent: Monday, June 24th 2:59 PM
Subject: RE: Already Rollin'!

Cliff –

Sorry for the delay. Couldn't get to your pages until the weekend. But I'm stoked, bro! Love the energy of this! Look, I can't get into a full response right now – Larry's just back from Europe (military boat across the channel, Red Cross plane from Paris, fucking wild) and we got a big meeting at three to talk about the entire slate – but four quick things:

1. Your geography is *totally* wack. I know London's the third fucking world but come on, crack a book or Google Earth or something.

2. It's HawksMOOR. And if you'd read the research material Craig got for you, you'd know he's not really the guy anyway. But I'll give you a get-out-of-jail-free on that one on the grounds of i) poetic license and ii) needing a cool-looking villain ;-)

3. Don't know if we can actually use the Plague Fleas. I know, I know. It blows. But apparently that info's like classified or shit.

4. Metallica? Really? Dude, the eighties called – they want their soundtrack back. Just busting your balls. This pretty much rocks. And you know what, I bet we *can* get Jonah Hill – I heard SUPER-BAD IV just fucking *died* at a test screening.

Scott

Sent from: ScottC@NewRidgeEntertainment.com
To: upstartcrow117@aol.com
Sent: Tuesday, June 25th 11:47 AM
Subject: RE: Already Rollin'!

Bad news, brother. I said I liked it and I was so not bullshitting you. I
still like it. But—don't hate me—I ran a drive-by verbal past Larry
and truth is he didn't really spark to it. Nothing to do with your
take, just that he really thinks that action-adventure isn't the way
to go with this material. I guess his eye-witness time in London
really made an impression on him. He's thinking high-road more
than popcorn now. When I get a better read on what he's planning
for us, I promise to bring you back into the loop. Okay?

Bestest,

Scott

Sent from: upstartcrow117@aol.com
To: ScottC@NewRidgeEntertainment.com
Sent: Tuesday, June 25th 3:33 PM
Subject: RE: Already Rollin'!

Sure, sure. Not a problem. Larry didn't break all those Box Office
records by *not* reading the zeitgeist well. I'm sure he's right about
the approach. But look. Let's not be too quick to spike this one in the
head. If it's *tone* that's the problem, we can reposition. Forget the
gags and the explosions. Look at the set-up and structure. How
about—just spit-balling here, go with me—how about if we made
Claire a documentarian (think Christiane Amanpour with a rockin'
bod) commissioned by Congress to capture on-the-ground footage of
the European situation. Yeah? And Jack is a former Black Ops guy
brought out of desk-job exile to keep her out of trouble? Maybe even
get an ersatz father-daughter vibe going between them? But sexual
tension, too, of course. Think Viggo Mortensen for Jack and for Claire

. . . shit, what's her name? That English Oscar-hottie? Carey Mulligan. Think about it. Whole different movie now. Popcorn schmopcorn. This is pure high road. Viggo all brooding and existentialist, Carey all oh-the-humanity. C'mon, bro, don't tell me *that* doesn't play.

Cliff

Sent from: ScottC@NewRidgeEntertainment.com
To: upstartcrow117@aol.com
Sent: Friday, June 28th 12:01 PM
Subject: RE: Already Rollin'!

Cliffie, you are a tryer. Gotta give you that. But I still think you're on a different page. You know what's big now? Reality.

Scott

Sent from: upstartcrow117@aol.com
To: ScottC@NewRidgeEntertainment.com
Sent: Friday, June 28th 4:52 PM
Subject: RE: Already Rollin'!

>>You know what's big now? Reality.<<

Alright. We can work with that. (You mean TV, right? And a series, not a special?) Check this out:

Who's for Lunch?
Reality/Competition
By Cliff Brightwell

Thirteen competitors. In a cage. Single walkway to a podium (think witness-box - whole set is like a Kafka courtroom). Beyond the podium, two doors. One marked EXIT, the other marked KITCHEN.

Tribunal of judges. You know – your classic JLo, Randy, Steven set-up. But dig this. The judges are *zombies*. You've heard they're talking now, right? Seen that amazing YouTube thing? Can't find the link, but just go to their search window and type in *ZombieGirl15*. You'll lose your lunch. But you'll smell the money. Anyway, so here's the twist. Our competitors *don't* want to be picked. Their gig is to present their cases for why the judges shouldn't eat them.

Sent from: ScottC@NewRidgeEntertainment.com
To: upstartcrow117@aol.com
Sent: Saturday, June 29th 11:28 AM
Subject: RE: Already Rollin'!

Can't believe I'm in the office on a Saturday fucking morning. I should be watching *Hannah Montana* reruns and trying to make the girlfriend believe I'm there for the comedy not the jailbait. But Larry's got us all in here around the clock right now. He's like a new man since he got back. He's making some changes around here and things are getting wack. Which is one reason I need you to be patient about your reality show idea. We're all learning to be careful about what we put on Larry's plate. Don't want to present it wrong and piss him off. Tell ya, the way he reacts these days, he makes Joel Silver look like a frigging pussycat.

Anyway, the good news is I think you're onto something here, young Clifford. It's an envelope-pusher, for sure, but since when was that a bad thing? Hang tough for a few and let me play with it, get the right spin. I wanna tweak it right, make sure Larry bites. More as soon as I know.

Scott

Sent from: upstartcrow117@aol.com
To: ScottC@NewRidgeEntertainment.com
Sent: Tuesday, July 2nd 3:13 PM
Subject: RE: Already Rollin'!

Scott. Just checking in. Haven't heard back from you on Larry's reaction to the reality show proposal. I'm cool with working it up a little more if that helps, but you have to let me know yay or nay. Fact is, my agent's up my ass to go directly to Fox with it, says they're desperate for a new franchise and that my idea could play as a ballsy response to the 'unfortunate incident' on that last *X Factor* out of London. God's honest truth, I'd much rather work with you guys than those assholes but, you know, trying to make a living here . . .

Sent from: upstartcrow117@aol.com
To: ScottC@NewRidgeEntertainment.com
Sent: Tuesday, July 2nd 5:59 PM
Subject: RE: Already Rollin'!

Hello?

Sent from: upstartcrow117@aol.com
To: ScottC@NewRidgeEntertainment.com
Sent: Wednesday, July 3rd 9:01 AM
Subject: RE: Already Rollin'!

What, are you guys dead, you don't answer your fucking e-mails?

Sent from: ScottC@NewRidgeEntertainment.com
To: upstartcrow117@aol.com
Sent: Wednesday, July 3rd 9:06 AM
Subject: RE: Already Rollin'!

Cliff,

Come in for meeting. Door always open. Eager to pick your brains.

Scott

THE MYSTERY

"For upwards of two hours, the sky was brilliant with lights"
—The Liverpool Daily Post, Sept 8th 1895

There's actually no mystery at all.

Not if you went the Bluey, anyway.

It used to be the grounds of a house, a big one. No Speke Hall or anything, but still technically a Stately Home. It had been called The Grange and was pulled down in May of 1895.

Four months later, minus an ornamental lake which had been filled in, the grounds were opened as a park for the children of Liverpool by the city council. It was officially named Wavertree Playground but was almost immediately dubbed 'The Mystery' by local people, because the person who bought the land and donated it to the city had asked for anonymity.

The Bluecoat School, a boys' Grammar, backed onto The Mystery and if you were a pupil there, even seventy-five years later, it was made pretty damn clear to you that it was one of our old Governors who'd forked up for the park. Philip Holt - one of our four school houses was named for him - was a maritime magnate in the days of the great ships and the Cast Iron Shore. The money needed to clear the land and create the park was probably no more than loose change to the man whose Blue Funnel Line practically owned the tea trade between Britain and China.

So. No mystery there.

I'll tell you what *was* a mystery, though. The fucking state of the Gents' bogs.

The Liverpool of the mid 'sixties was a city suffering a dizzying drop into recession. No more ships, no more industry, no more Beatles – *Tara, mum. Off to London to shake the world. Don't wait up* – but even so, the public toilets at the northwest corner of the Mystery were astonishingly disgusting. 'Derelict' didn't even come close. They'd been neither bricked up nor pulled down. It was more like they'd been simply forgotten, as if a file had been lost somewhere in the town hall and nobody with any responsibility knew they even existed. Utterly unlooked after in a third world sort of way and alarming to enter, let alone use. No roof, no cubicle doors, no paper, what was left of the plaster over the ancient red bricks completely covered with graffiti of an obsessive and sociopathic nature, and last mopped out sometime before Hitler trotted into Poland.

But, you know, if you had to go you had to go, and I'd had many a piss there back in the day. If you didn't actually touch anything, you had a fighting chance of walking out without having contracted a disease.

But to see that soiled shed-like structure still there on an autumn afternoon thirty years later was more than a little surprising.

I had some business to attend to and shouldn't really have allowed myself to be distracted, but I felt a need to check it out. The boys appeared just as I approached the stinking moss-scarred walkway entrance.

There were two of them, both about thirteen, though one at least a head taller than his friend. Although they weren't actually blocking the path – standing just off to the side, ankle-deep in the overgrown grass – they nevertheless gave the impression of being self-appointed sentries, as if they were there to perhaps collect a toll or something.

"Where are you going, then?" The first one said. His hair was russet and looked home-cut and his face was patchily rosy with the promise of acne.

"The bog," I said.

They looked at each other, and then back at me.

"*This* bog?" said the first.

"Fuckin' 'ell," said the second. He was the shorter one, black Irish pale, unibrowed and sullen.

"You don't wanna go in *there*," said the first.

"Why would you go in *there*?" said his mate.

I shrugged, but I wasn't sure they noticed. They were staring at me with the kind of incipient aggression you'd expect, but weren't actually meeting my eyes. Instead, they were both looking at me at about mid-chest height, as if looking at someone smaller and younger.

"Why wouldn't I?" I said.

"He might get ya," said the black-haired one.

"Who?"

"The feller," said the redhead.

"What feller?" I asked him.

He looked surprised. "Yerav'n 'eard of 'im?" he said.

"No."

"Fuckin' 'ell," said the shorter one.

"He's there all the time," his friend said. "Nights, mostly."

"Yeah," Blackie nodded in support. "Nights."

"Yeah?" I said to the taller one, the redhead, who seemed to be the boss. "What does he do?"

"Waits there for lads," he said.

"What for?"

"You know."

I didn't. He shook his head off my blank look, in pity for my ignorance. "He bums them," he said.

"Shags them up the bum," said his companion helpfully.

"Why?"

"Fuckin' 'ell," said the first one, and looked at his friend with a *we've got a right idiot here* expression. "Because he's an 'omo, that's why."

"A Hom," said the second.

The first looked thoughtful. Came to a decision. "We better go in with ya," he said.

"For safety, like," said the second, with only a trace of his eagerness betraying itself. "He might be in there now."

"Oh, I think I'll be alright," I said. "If he's in there, I'll tell him I'm not in the mood."

My tone was confusing to them. It wasn't going the way it was meant to, the way it perhaps usually did.

"Yeah, burrit's worse than we said," the first one told me, as if worried some opportunity was slipping away. He looked to his friend. "Tell him about the, you know, the thing."

"Yeah, he's gorra nutcracker," Blackie said. "You know warramean?" He mimed a plier-like action in order to help me visualise what he was talking about. "After he's bummed ya, he crushes yer bollocks."

I remembered that. It was a story I'd first heard when I was much younger than them. An urban legend, though the phrase hadn't been coined at the time, conjured into being in the summer of 1965 and believed by nearly every nine year old boy who heard it.

They were still looking at my chest, as if staring down a smaller contemporary.

"How old am I?" I asked them.

"You wha'?" the redhead said.

"How old do you think I am?"

They shared a look, and the taller one shrugged. "Dunno," he said. "About eight?"

"Might be ten," the other one said, not to me but to his friend, and the redhead shot him an angry look as if he didn't want to be bothered with details or sidetracked by debate.

I snapped my fingers loudly, close to my face, and drew their eyes upwards.

They looked confused. Their eyes weren't quite focussing on mine, and I still wasn't sure they could really see me. There was something else hovering behind their confusion; an anxiety, perhaps, as if they feared they might be in trouble, as if something would know they were being distracted from their duty and wouldn't be very pleased with them. As far as they were concerned, this was a day like every other and *needed* to be a day like every other, and any disruption in the pattern was alarming to them, in however imprecise a way.

I didn't doubt that this was how they'd spent a fair portion of their time, back when it was linear. Having a little chat and preparing some eight year old victim for a good battering. They'd probably done it before, and more than once. Done it regularly, perhaps, until their belief in the very predator they used as bait had become their undoing.

"Take a look at this," I said and took something out of my pocket to show them.

A few minutes later, back on the main footpath, I took a look back over my shoulder. It was very dark now and neither the toilets nor the boys were anywhere in sight. The moon had risen in the cloudless sky and I took a glance at my watch. It was an old fashioned watch and its dial was un-illuminated, but I was fairly certain it said it was still four in the afternoon.

I'd kept up a brisk pace while checking the time and, when I looked up again, the house was directly ahead of me, though I hadn't noticed it earlier. Its size alone suggested it was probably magnificent in the daylight, but its lawns were unlit and its windows shuttered and it appeared simply as a great black shape, a mass of deeper darkness against the midnight blue of the sky.

Just outside its black iron gates, half-open as if in tentative invitation, a little girl was standing on the gravel of the driveway.

She was dressed in a simple knee-length smock dress and didn't look up at me as I walked towards her. She was concentrating on her game, her mouth opening and closing in recitation of something. It was a skipping song, as best I remembered it, but she was using it as accompaniment for the rapid bouncing of a small rubber ball between the gravel and her outstretched palm.

"Dip dip dip,
My blue ship.
Sailing on the water
Like a cup and saucer.
O, U, T spells—"

Oh, that's right. Not a skipping song at all. A rhyme of selection or exclusion, a variant of eeny meeny miney mo. The little girl, long and ringleted hair pulled back from her forehead by a wide black ribbon, seemed to remember that at the same moment I did and, just as she mouthed the word *out*, her hand snapped shut around the ball, her eyes flicked up to meet mine, and she thrust her other hand out to point its index finger dramatically at me. Her eyes were jet black and her now silent mouth was pulled in a tight unsmiling line.

"I'm out?" I asked her.

She didn't say anything, and nor did her fixed expression waver. I let the silence build for a few moments as we stared at each other, though I blinked deliberately several times to let her know that if it was a contest it was one she was welcome to win.

"Your concentration's slipping," I said eventually. "Where did the ball go?"

Her little brow furrowed briefly and she looked down at her empty hand. She pulled an annoyed face and then looked back at me.

"Are you going into the house?" she asked.

"In a manner of speaking," I said.

She gave a small tut of derision. "Is that supposed to be clever?" she said.

"No," I said. "Not really."

"Good," she said. "Because it's *not* clever. It's just stupid. Are you going into the house or not?"

"The house isn't really here," I told her.

"Then where are you standing?" she said. "And who are you talking to?"

Without waiting for an answer, she began to lean her head sideways and down. Keeping her unblinking eyes fixed on mine, she continued the movement, slowly and steadily, with no apparent difficulty or discomfort, until her pale little cheek rested flat against her right shoulder and her head was at an impossible right-angle to her neck. At the same time, in some strange counterpoint, her hair rose up into the air, stately and unhurried, until the ringlets were upright and taut, quivering against the darkness like mesmerised snakes dancing to an unheard piper.

I grinned at her. She was good at this.

We exchanged a few more words before I walked through the gates without her, following the wide and unbending path to the house itself. The imposingly large front door was as unlit as the rest of the exterior and was firmly closed. But I knew that others had come to this house before me, and that the door, despite its size and its weight and its numerous locks, had opened as easily for them as it would for me.

The rest of the vast reception room was pretty impressive, but the portrait over the fireplace was magnificent.

The picture itself was at least eight feet tall, allowing for some grass below and some sky above its life-size and black-suited central figure, who stared out into the room with the confident Victorian swagger of those born to wealth and empire. A foxhound cowered low at its master's feet and, in the far background, which appeared to be the grounds of the house, a group of disturbingly young children were playing Nymphs and Shepherds.

The room, like the long hall along which I'd walked to come to it, was illuminated by many candles, though I'd yet to see anyone who might have lit them. Through a half-open door at the far end of the room, though, I could see a shadow flicking back and forth, back and forth, as if somebody was about their business in a repeated pattern of movements.

As I came into the ante-room, the young woman who was pacing up and down looked up briefly from the clipboard she was holding. She appeared to be barely twenty, dressed in what I guessed to be the kind of nurse's uniform women might have worn when they were dressing wounds received in the Crimea, and the stern prettiness of her face and the darkness of her eyes said she could have been an older sister of the little girl I'd met outside the gates.

There was a single bed in the room and, though it was unoccupied, its sheets were rumpled, as if the woman's patient had just recently gone for a little walk. There were wires and cables and drip-feeds lying on the sheets and the other ends of some of them were connected to a black and white television monitor that attempted to hide its anachronism by being cased within a brass and mahogany housing of a Victorian splendour and an H. G. Wells inventiveness.

The young woman, having registered my presence with neither surprise nor welcome, was back to her job of glancing at the monitor and then marking something on her clipboard.

The image on the monitor – grainy and distorted, washed-out like a barely-surviving kinescope of some long ago transmission – was a fixed-angle image of moonlight-bathed waves, deep-water waves, no shore in sight, as if a single camera were perched atop an impossible tower standing alone in some vast and distant ocean.

I looked at the image for a moment or two while she continued to pace and to make checkmarks on her clipboard.

"So what does that do?" I asked eventually, nodding at the monitor.

She stopped pacing and turned to look at me again. Her expression, while not unfriendly, was conflicted, as if she were both grateful for the break in routine and mildly unsettled by it.

"It used to show his dreams," she said, and turned her head briefly to look again at the endless and unbreaking waves. "But it's empty now."

She looked back at me and tilted her head a little, like she was deciding if I was safe enough to share a confidence with. "It's frightening, isn't it?" she said.

"Frightening?" I said. "I don't know. Perhaps it just means he's at peace."

"No, no," she said, her voice rising in a kind of nervous excitement. "You've misunderstood. That isn't what I meant." And then she caught herself and her voice went flat as if she feared lending emotion to what she said next. "I mean we might be having his dreams *for* him."

She looked at me half-expectantly, her eyes wide, like she was hoping I might tell her that she was wrong, but before I could answer a bell began to ring from a room somewhere deeper in the house.

"Teatime," she said. "You'd best hurry."

The children sat at trestle tables and ate without enthusiasm and there were far too many of them.

Their clothes were a snapshot history lesson; tracksuits and trainers, pullovers and short pants, britches and work-shirts, smocks and knickerbockers. The ones who'd been here longest were an unsettling monochrome against the colours of the more recent arrivals, and it wasn't only their outfits that were fading to grey.

Despite the dutiful shovelling of gruel into their mouths, I knew that they weren't hungry – there was only one inhabitant of this house who was hungry – and I wondered briefly why they even needed to pretend to eat, but figured that habit and routine were part of what helped him chain them here. Not a one of them spoke. Not a one of them smiled. I decided against joining them and headed back down the corridor to which the nurse had pointed me.

I saw something unspeakable in one of the rooms I passed and felt no need to look in any of the others.

The reception room was still empty when I got there. Patience is encouraged in these situations but, you know, fuck it. I decided to break something. There was an exquisite smoked glass figurine resting on top of the piano. I didn't even pick it up, just swept it away with the back of my hand and listened to it shatter against the parquet floor.

I hadn't intended to look, but a rapid skittering caught my eye and I bent down, barely in time to see a tiny something, wretched and limbless, slithering wetly beneath the sofa. I was still crouched down when there was a noise from somewhere behind me, unusually loud for what it most sounded like; the sticky gossamer ripping of a blunder through an unseen spider's web.

I stood up quickly, turning around to look. There was still nobody in the room but, though the large picture over the fireplace was intact and undamaged, its central figure was missing.

"You're a little older than my usual guests," the master of the house said from immediately behind me.

I span back around, very successfully startled. There was nothing overtly threatening about his posture, but he was standing uncomfortably close to me and I wasn't at all fond of his smile.

"A little older," he repeated. "But I'm sure we can find you a room."

"I won't be staying," I said. My voice was steady enough, but I was pissed off at how much he'd thrown me and pissed off more at how much he'd enjoyed it.

"You're very much mistaken," he said. "My house is easy to enter but not so easy to leave."

I understood his confidence. He had a hundred years of experience to justify his thinking that I was one of his usual guests. He could see me, so I had to be dead. Just as most ghosts are invisible to people, most people are invisible to ghosts. But, just as there are a few anomalous ghosts who *can* be seen by people, so are there a few anomalous people who can be seen by ghosts. And he'd just met one.

"Do you know what this is?" I said, and brought the tesseract out of my pocket. They've been standard issue at the department for the last couple of years. Fuck knows where they get them made, but I have a feeling it isn't Hong Kong.

I let it rest in my palm and he looked at it. He tried to keep his expression neutral but I could tell his curiosity was piqued. It always is.

"What does it do?" he said.

"Well, it doesn't really *do* anything," I said. "It just is."

"And what do you want me to do about it?"

"Nothing," I said. "Just look at it for a while."

I gave it a little tap and it slid impossibly through itself.

The room shivered in response, but I don't think he noticed. His eyes were fixed on the little cube and its effortless dance through dimensions.

"There's something wrong with it," he said, but the tone of his voice was fascinated rather than dismissive. "I can't see it properly."

"It's difficult," I agreed. "Because part of it shouldn't be here. Doesn't mean it's not real. Just means it doesn't belong in the space it's in."

The metaphor hit home, as it always did. I don't know why the tesseract works so well on them – I mean, it's utterly harmless, more wake-up call than weapon – but it's definitely made the job easier. He looked up at me. His face was already a little less defined than it had been, but I could still read the fear in it. He was smart, though. Went straight for the important questions and fuck the nuts and bolts.

"Will I be judged?" he said.

"Nobody's judged."

"Will I be hurt?"

"Nobody's hurt."

"Will I be—" He stopped himself then, as an unwilled understanding came to him, and he repeated what he'd just said. Same words. Different stress. "Will I *be*?"

I looked at him.

"Nobody'll be." I said.

It was too late for him to fight, but the animal rage for identity made him try, his imagined flesh struggling against its dissolution and his softening arms reaching out for me uselessly.

"You know who hangs around?" I said. "People with too little will of their own, and people with too much. Let it go. We're just lights in the sky, and their shadows."

"I'll miss it!" he shouted, his disappearing mouth twisting into a final snarl of appetite and terror.

"You won't miss a thing," I said, and watched him vanish.

I'd been in there longer than I thought and, as I walked back through the park towards the Hunter's Lane gate, true night was falling. But it was far from dark. There'd been so many souls in the house, young and old, predator and prey, that the cascade of their dissolution was spectacular and sustained.

For upwards of two hours, the sky was brilliant with lights.

Like an anniversary. Like a half remembered dream. Like a mystery.

AVIATRIX

- 1 -

Way he figured it was this. You go up in one of those things, it's going to crash. It crashes, you're going to die. You're going to die, what the hell's stopping you from going to Stan's Corner Donuts in Westwood Village three hours before check-in at LAX and eating your way through five Maple Bars? Shit, you'd be cinders and memory long before that superlative sweetness transformed itself into inches and artery-closure so who cared?

- 2 -

He actually settled for three. He wasn't hedging his bets on survival or anything, it was just that three really were enough. Finishing the third, filling his mouth with the last two inches of maple-flavoured frosting and soft warm dough, was the optimum point of pleasure. Starting another would undercut the sensual perfection. Better to stop. But God, they were good. Sugar and fat. It didn't get any better. The Western World had reached apotheosis at the moment that combinations of those two foodstuffs became readily available to anyone with half an income. Keep your Beethoven. Fuck your Goya. Sugar and Fat. That was culture.

'You wanna refill on the coffee, Steve?'

Dyson looked over his shoulder to the counter. His name wasn't Steve but he was the only customer in there so he figured it was him who was being asked.

'No. No thanks. I'm fine.'

The guy behind the counter – young, long-haired, loud shirt – grinned.

'Can't be fine, Steve. Three donuts. Gotta be some kind of oral compensation going on.'

Dyson (still not Steve, still Jonathan) hesitated. He'd always hated people guessing things about him, hated more the readiness of some strangers to break the social contract of silence with which we surround such guesses. Nevertheless, he answered. Probably because he also hated appearing to care.

'Flying,' he said, 'hate it. Every time I *know* I'm going to die.'

'And every time you haven't.'

'God's oversight. Or his little joke.'

'False sense of security thing?'

'Something like that.'

'Get you to where you think maybe, just maybe, this is gonna be alright then – *bam!* Gotcha! Yeah?'

'Something like that.'

'Don't wanna burst your bubble, Steve ... but you're probably not that important. Know what I mean?'

'Oh, I don't feel special or anything. I...'

'You figure the joke's on all of us. "As flies to wanton boys are we to the gods. They kill us for their sport." *Macbeth*.'

'*Lear*.'

'What?'

'It's *Lear. King Lear*. Not *Macbeth*.'

'Oh. Whatever. It's still bullshit. They've got better things to do.'

'Yeah?'

'Yeah. Like watching us learn to fly. And being proud of us'

Dyson paused before replying, filling the silence by draining his cup of what little coffee remained. He looked over the Styrofoam lip at the counterman, at his flawless young face, at his open smile. He didn't need this. He came to Stan's for donuts not facile New Age optimism. Worse; he'd conversed. Next time he came in and this guy was working there was a ready-made opening for more conversation. He hated that. Donuts were private. Stan's was ruined for him.

He put the cup down beside the wax-paper and crumpled napkins, mumbled a mock high-spirited hope-you're-right-see-ya, hefted up his on-flight bag, and left. It was only when he reached the taxi-rank at the corner of Westwood and Lindbrook that he realised he'd assumed there would be a 'next time' at Stan's. The sudden anger he felt at the counterman for tricking him into such an expectation was subsumed in the nauseating warmth of the anxiety rush that flooded his system as punishment for hope. His legs were weak as he grinned inanely at the driver of the first cab in line and let himself into the back seat.

'Hi. Howya doin'?' he said in response to the driver's enquiring eyes in the rear-view mirror, 'LAX please.'

- 3 -

Dyson was always very strict with himself about when he could take the Valium. Before check-in was no good – you might find out there that the flight was delayed and thus have wasted one of the precious little pills (increasingly harder to get because stupid doctors thought beta-blockers were healthier. Healthier! *Who fucking cares?*) – but, equally, you didn't want to wait too long after getting your boarding pass – take-off was the worst part and God forbid you should be hurtled down that runway still waiting for the drug to kick in, embarrassing yourself and disturbing other passengers with your moans and copious sweating. No, there was a five or ten minute window immediately after check-in during which a bar could be found, a large scotch on the rocks ordered, a ten-milligram placed on the tongue, and the liquor swallowed in a single gulp carrying the pill with it.

Dyson had done all that and was now strapped in his window seat pretending to read the airline's magazine. He glanced at his watch. Take-off was in fifteen minutes. But he wasn't waiting for take-off. He was waiting for that first evidence of the drug's efficacy, the half-sleep he always fell into immediately before the plane taxied. *Mustn't prompt it,* he thought, and looked back down at the article on French street-markets.

Apparently you could buy groceries there. And occasionally clothes. Sometimes prints. How fucking riveting. The disembodied voice of a cabin crew member began advising passengers about the safety features to be found on this 767. Several of the bookstalls by the Seine sold English paperbacks. In the unlikely event of an emergency, wine was much cheaper than in the cafes. There were several exits near the market and clothes could be found under the banks of the river in front of you. The child by the bookstall was clearly indicated and even though oxygen was flowing would not inflate. Beside the river, far from the boy, was a woman who was speaking. People were walking by, not even noticing her strange manner of dress. She was clad in a bulky fur-lined leather jacket and had a tight-fitting leather helmet on her head, its fastened straps hanging on either side of her face.

Dyson wanted to hear what she was saying and walked nearer to her. She smiled at his approach and continued her explanation even as she motioned for him to climb in the open seat behind the one in which she sat.

'Static is occasionally encountered on the radios of Heaven.'

Her voice was confident and benign. Dyson fastened the belt around his waist and adjusted his goggles. He looked beyond the jarring geometries of the struts between the upper and lower sets of wood-and-canvas wings to the undisturbed green fields on either side of the sandy runway. The fields, perfectly flat, stretched to every horizon. He, the woman, and the biplane itself were the only foreign objects. It was important that they left.

The woman turned round in her seat to smile at him again.

'We must discover the horizontal movement of elevators,' she said and, turning away from him once more, started up the plane s small engine, sending the single front-mounted propeller spinning furiously. Transmuted by the propeller's frenzy, the formerly still air whipped back across Dyson's face as an intimate and exhilarating wind. He opened his mouth to it, excited, and placed his hands on either side of the narrow open cockpit as the plane began to rush forward across the sand. The runway was uneven and bumpy but Dyson felt no fear as the fragile bi-plane hurtled faster and faster along it. The machine and the moment were implicit with flight, pregnant with escape. The trajectory held no potential other than a leap into the sky and the freedom of the winds.

Dyson wondered how he could hear the pilot's voice against the combined roaring of engine and air, but hear it he did.

'You need to put your seat in the upright position,' she seemed to be saying, though he could see only her back and the waves of corn-blonde hair that hung below the back of her helmet. He looked down at himself. The seat was welded in position tight against the cockpit. How could he move it? He closed his eyes to think about this further.

'Sir? Your seat has to be upright for take-off.'

Dyson opened his eyes. A dark-haired flight attendant was smiling apologetically at him as she stood in the aisle beside the seat of the passenger next to him.

'I'm sorry,' she stressed, stretching the word out to demonstrate further her distress at disturbing him, 'but the captain's about to take off and I need your seat to be upright.'

Dyson nodded vigorously and blinked himself more thoroughly awake.

'Of course, of course,' he said and pressed the button in the armrest beside him, leaning from the waist as he did so to allow the seat-back to inch forward into its take-off position.

'Thank you,' the stewardess said, rewarding him with another smile before moving on to check the seat-positions of other passengers.

Dyson hadn't lowered his seat consciously. He'd never do that. He always fastened his seat-belt immediately he sat down, too. He hated having to be asked or reminded about either of those things. One of the masks he wore to hide his terror was the seasoned, bored-with-the-ritu-als, flier and he hated to be caught out. His thigh must have pressed against the button as he dozed and lowered his seat-back in his sleep. He looked out of his window. The plane had left the gate and was swinging round onto the designated runway to begin its launch. A wave of anxiety went through him, small (the Valium was doing its job) but unpleasant enough. He was furious with his thigh. He'd really been asleep, so asleep that maybe for the first time he could have gotten through take-off unconscious and woken only when the plane had already reached cruising altitude. That would have been great. But no, here he was as usual – convinced of death and powerless to do anything about it as the huge machine (*too big. Too heavy. How could these things fly? How could they?*) thundered its way toward immolation. He sat bolt upright, tense in every muscle, conscious of every breath, and waited for the inevitable catastrophe.

- 4 -

Dyson finished his cognac and settled back a little in his seat. He felt a lot better now. The plane had been at a steady 31,000 feet for over an hour and all the banking and turning that made the first twenty minutes of any flight the worst were long over. Dyson had had two scotches before dinner, a red wine to accompany the filet mignon, and a cognac to accompany the coffee. And the Byrds were on one of the in-flight audio channels, the falling bass-line and soaring harmonies of 'Turn, Turn, Turn' entering each of Dyson's ears and meeting somewhere in the middle of his head.

He often experienced these twenty or thirty minute stretches of euphoria during a flight, times where he could gaze out of his window at the distant landscapes below him and feel genuinely good about being up in a plane. But it took a lot of alcohol to get him in such states and it took very little to get him out of them; ten seconds of turbulence was enough, or the sight of another plane through his window (distance and direction didn't matter – if there were two plane's in the same cubic mile of air, he assumed they would find each other). But the Byrds and the booze and the unshaky sky had given him this period of peace and he luxuriated in it.

Over on the video monitor a couple of rows in front of him he could see actors mouthing words and buildings exploding silently. He wondered about tuning his headset to the movie soundtrack but decided against it. He closed his eyes instead, turned the music down slightly, and stretched his legs out as much as he could beneath the seat in front of him.

The sea below them was a pale purple. They'd left the glass mountains and their strange shifting subterranean contents long behind them, though the aviatrix had dipped the biplane sufficiently at the time for Dyson to catch a glimpse of one huge clouded eye the size of a shopping-mall parking-lot which had blinked beneath the crystal as they'd buzzed past. Dyson was more impressed with the waves though; with no shore to break against save gravity, they rose in the middle of their ocean, losing their colour as they did so, to climb vertically in towering translucency and foam themselves into a fury of deep-white dissolution at their skyscraper-high peaks.

Occasionally, his pilot would turn half-round in her front seat to smile at him and to gesture with a directional hand at some other point of interest. They'd been flying for hours, it seemed, and Dyson felt he could fly forever. His pilot was beautiful and the sights they shared were wonderful. He was reaching forward to tap her shoulder and tell her this when a sharp pinging noise somewhere above his head distracted him and made him look up.

He found that he was looking at an illuminated sign telling him to fasten his seat-belt. For a moment he was terribly confused and then a quick glance around him reminded him of where he was. His seat-belt of course was still fastened but the heavy-set man beside him needed to fish the two halves of his belt out from beneath his expansive backside and clip them together. The senior flight attendant's voice emerged from the overhead speakers in the cabin to reinforce the instruction.

'Ladies and gentlemen, the Captain has found it necessary to illuminate the seat-belt signs while we go through this turbulence. If you are standing anywhere in the cabin, please return to your seats. Thank you.'

Dyson's heart beat a little faster. The plane was bumping and rocking like an express train on a bad stretch of track. He dropped that simile bloody quickly; derailment here didn't mean ploughing up some farmer's field, it meant a drop. A big drop. Thirty. One. Thousand. Feet. *Stop it, stop it*, he told himself. Turbulence, that's all. Very normal. Very ordinary. He looked at his watch. Good. The flight was well past the halfway point – which probably meant nothing aeronautically but was always a good psychological signpost for him. He tried to summon up the feeling he had had in his dream in which flight was not only a miracle but an ecstasy. He failed of course but at least it gave him something to think about as the plane rode out the wind.

The dream from which he'd just awoken was plainly a continuation of the one he'd had immediately before take-off. That was very strange. He'd never re-entered a dream before. The nearest he'd had to even a recurring dream was on those few occasions that he woke feeling that he'd visited places in the night which were geographically close to places he'd dreamed in before – as if somehow his night-time self might sometime meet a dream cartographer who would lay out for him route-marked maps demonstrating that this dream of a Tuesday in March ten years ago took place about four blocks from this one of a recent July and that both were only a short cab-ride from the nightmare of December last.

This dream, though, felt like it had continued while he was busy being awake and that he had rejoined it after an elapsed time equivalent to the time he had spent away. Very strange – it gave the dream state an equal standing with the waking one that he had never before granted to it. It was as if he was waking from each into the other, moving between equally valid territories rather than simply being entertained by his unconscious.

He thought of the woman in his dream and her romantically anachronistic dress. He recognised the provenance of the imagery of course – those 1930's women fliers whose likenesses he had seen in magazine photos and documentary footage – but the aviatrix of his unconscious was something more than them. She was the paradigm of them all, the missing original from which they had been cast. It was as if he had dreamed of Amelia Earheart and dreamed not of the living woman who had disappeared during her last flight but of her spirit, of her principle, of the *idea* of which she had been simply the symbol.

His dreaming self had fashioned her into an Amelia Earheart who was never lost, but *translated* – an Amelia Earheart who had flown herself through the clouds of unknowing into a yonder never so blue nor so wild. Not lost, but escaped; flying forever across imagination's skies; borne on the secret winds that blow above the dream country.

Another *ping* from above his head stopped his analysis. He looked up. The seat-belt light had gone out. Dyson felt a rush of pleasure. She was still piloting him, it seemed; his thoughts of her had taken him through the turbulence into calmer skies without his usual neurotic attention to every second and every shudder.

He smiled. He missed her, he realised. He wondered where they were and over what wonders she was flying him while he was away. Would it be possible to go back? Could he *will* himself into that territory into which he had previously merely stumbled? Excited, he fished through the seat-pocket for the in-flight courtesy bag and pulled out the complimentary eye-mask. On his rare forays up and down the aisles of aircraft on which he'd flown he'd always thought the passengers wearing those things looked inordinately fucking stupid but now he didn't give a shit what he looked like and he slipped the elasticated strap over his head and leaned back in his seat.

'Aviatrix,' he said silently, relishing the word like a mantra or a spell of summoning. 'Aviatrix.'

- 6 -

The desert was sentient.

It lay beneath them, an expanse of subtly shifting sands, and Dyson, looking behind him, could see no beginning to its hugeness and, looking ahead, could see no end. What he could see, however, was that the desert observed their flight just as much as they observed it. For the most part its observation was implicit – a sensed thing rather than a seen – but occasionally, in a spirit of inquiry, it would reform part of itself, sending up into the air vast sheets of sand that would rise with breathtaking speed on either side of the biplane so that where a moment before they had been high above a plain they were suddenly flying low between the towering walls of a valley, walls that shimmered with the constant movement of their countless grains.

Once, it even completed the canopy, curving the tops of its walls toward each other until they met so that Dyson and the aviatrix were flying within a tunnel, a tunnel that should have been lightless but was somehow not – as if the desert had widened the spaces between every tiny grain of itself to allow its visitors the luxury of sight.

They followed the tunnel for several minutes before the desert fell back around them to its passive state below. The woman turned in her cockpit to look at Dyson. Her hands were off the controls but he had realised some time back that she didn't really need physical contact with the machinery. She and the plane were essentially one. They drove themselves through these dream skies by desire, not science.

'Thunder has three sides, Steve,' she said, 'but no Dalmatians.'

Dyson nodded. He was beginning to understand her. And was already terribly in love. She nodded downwards and he looked to see.

They were flying over a hole in the world. Bounded like a Midwest lake by long shore-roads, what Dyson saw was no body of water but a jet-black expanse of deep space, studded with distant stars and cloudy filaments of gases.

The roar of an explosion suddenly deafened him. He couldn't understand for a moment. He could see nothing that had happened that would explain the sound. Then he heard a voice to his side screaming in terminal panic.

'Jesus fucking Christ! The wing's gone!'

- 7 -

Dyson, already screaming himself, tore the eye-mask from his face with fingers tingling with prescient terror.

The fat man in the seat beside him was twitching like a speared beast, arms flapping uselessly in the air, the stink of his voided bowels invading Dyson's senses almost before anything else.

Dyson, unaware of the whimpers and screams coming from his own mouth, swept the cabin with his eyes. People were ripping themselves free of their restraining belts and clambering pointlessly into the aisles. There was nothing they could do for themselves but they were listening to a primal voice within that decreed movement even when movement couldn't save them.

One flight attendant was paying lip service to procedure and shouting out for the passengers to remain calm while her colleagues, knowing it was over, joined in the atavistic dance of the civilians, running, scrambling, stumbling, screaming. The howls of the doomed filled the cabin of the aircraft and for one precious fleeting second Dyson had an absurd sense of satisfaction. He'd always known this terror – at least in embryo – and now that, fully born, it was running rampant through the souls of the previously complacent, he felt the poisoned vindication of the doomsayer.

It was all of three seconds since the exploding engine had torn the wing from the 767 and, incredibly, apart from the shuddering lurch to the side that accompanied the sundering, the crippled plane had stayed more or less steady.

That stopped being true.

Nose first, it dropped like a stone.

Dyson's belt was still fastened around him. It hurt like fuck as all his weight pressed against it. The passengers who had found the time to snap their belts, though, fell screaming down the vertical chute that the cabin of the plane had become and smashed into the first solid objects that barred their way. Eight people died before the plane hit the ground. Twenty-three people wished they had. One hundred and fifty more were beyond thought, pushed howling into a primal state of animal terror.

Dyson was one of them. He was squealing like a three-day torture victim. There was nothing in his mind except dread and denial and nothing in his body save ice and emptiness. Nothing could save him and nothing did.

The plane arrowed itself into the unyielding rock of a mountain range and, fuel tanks still one third full, exploded instantly into all-consuming fire, killing everyone on board.

- 8 -

Dyson had been screaming the second before he died and was surprised to find he was still screaming the second after. He was still falling at a nauseating speed, as if the mountain and the explosion had not interrupted him at all. He was no longer in his seat, however, and no longer in the plane. It was just him, falling through complete blackness and screaming.

By the time a minute had passed, though, continuing to scream seemed a little stupid. And so he stopped. The blackness was still all around him and there seemed to be little he could do about that except continue to fall through it. Unless of course he opened his eyes. And so he did.

The sky was jade-green and tasted moist and slightly acidic. Far below, the ground was writhing. It was a mass of intertwined wormlike creatures, each the length of Europe and all of them the colours of bruising. Immediately in front of him, and falling just as fast, was the aviatrix.

Dyson tried to reach out to her but found it difficult to move his limbs against the rush of air. It was unnecessary. She turned toward him, riding the air like a skydiver, and took hold of his hand. Instantly, their fall stopped. Dyson gasped. They were hovering in midair. Her eyes locked on his and he found himself unable to look away as her change began.

- 9 -

Above the unending territories of the dream country the great white bird flew as she had always flown, her vast shadow bringing night in her wake.

Invisible from the ground, in the warmth of that huge snowy breast, nestled Dyson, fingers clinging happily to the feathers of the white goddess as her great wings beat tireless against the skies and flew into forever.

THE LAST OF THE
INVISIBLE KINGS

" I am the voice whose sound is manifold
And the word whose appearance is multiple.
I am the utterance of my name."
– The Thunder (from the Gnostic Gospels)

She hardly saw them coming.

Two young men, big and wide. One of them arguably fat, rather than muscular. But tough fat. Hard fat. Nothing cuddly about it.

Sweetest smile on one of them, though. The one who asked her for the money.

It was two-thirty in the morning and Sophie had been alone on the single-track platform for more than twenty minutes. The silent emptiness of the unmanned Amtrak station had surprised her when the taxi had dropped her off. I mean, middle of the night and all, and High Point, North Carolina was hardly London or Paris, but still – no porter, no ticket-seller, no staff at all? No one to even confirm that she was in the right place, no one to assure this friendly little English stranger that very soon the northbound train – the gleaming silver *Crescent*, out of New Orleans – would arrive for her, show her to her sleeper compartment, and carry her through the night, in an opulence unattainable by airlines, to New York city.

That was why she was taking the train in the first place, for the romance and the adventure. Well, that and the fact she was shit-scared of flying. Turned out, though, that she wasn't that fond of sitting alone in a deserted train station in the early hours of the morning, either. The station was bang in the middle of High Point's historic downtown, but High Point's historic downtown was just as deserted as its station. Since her taxi had pulled away, Sophie hadn't heard even a single car-engine.

The station, though sunk a flight below street level and reached by steep stone steps from the access road above, was completely open to the cloudless and star-studded night. Which meant at least she could smoke. And truth was that after twenty minutes and a couple of ciggies she'd actually begun to enjoy the dream-like strangeness of the situation. So alone, so unattended; as if, in a brief moment of inattention, she had magically stepped out of life into a limbo of stasis and midnight silence, a curiously comfortable limbo, clean and well-maintained and – perhaps most importantly – one in reassuring proximity to the gleaming steel tracks along which, at any moment now, the world would hurtle back to claim her and re-admit her to its quotidian chaos of people and noise and life and movement. It was already becoming a story she could look forward to telling once she was back home in England, one small example of the exoticism and mystery she had managed to find in America.

Of course, Sophie was still seeing any story she might tell as a one-woman show at that point. Upon the unexpected arrival of her fellow cast members, she was suddenly less sanguine about the type of story it was going to be.

The boys must have walked to the station, because the first indication Sophie had of their arrival was the sound of their feet coming down the steps. They advanced a few yards along the platform, stopping slightly short of the single bench on which Sophie sat. She looked up at them and smiled. Small smile. Careful smile. Friendly, but not too welcoming.

One of them, the one not gripping the zippered black hold-all, gave her a slight nod in return. The other one turned to stand looking out at the track, not acknowledging her at all.

They were younger than her by a couple of years, Sophie figured. Still in their teens. "Is this the right platform for the *Crescent*?" she said. "The New York train?"

The one with the bag snapped at her. "Think we work for the Railroad?" Still didn't turn his head toward her.

Sophie heard the challenging resentment in his voice. They were indeed the first black people she'd seen in the three days she'd been in High Point, but that wasn't what she'd meant at all.

"No," she said. "No, of course not. I just thought you might know. There's no one here to help."

Fuck. She wished she hadn't added that last part.

The other boy – the shorter but wider one, the one who'd at least nodded a greeting – cocked his head at the sound of her voice. He was wearing a windcheater with the word *Knicks* on it. He smiled. A sweet smile, shyly intrigued.

"Where you from?" he said. "Australia?"

Sophie shook her head. "England," she said, and fought back the protective but loathsomely patronizing desire to add that her best friend at high school had been a black girl. "Are you from here? High Point, I mean. Not America. Obviously you're from America."

"New York," he said, as if astonished that she couldn't tell.

The taller one half-turned. Plainly the close-mouthed alpha-dog to Knicks's chatty puppy, Sophie almost expected him to call his friend into line, order him to stop talking. Instead, he looked down near Sophie's feet, at the two stubbed-out cigarette butts. She stared at the tell-tale lipstick traces on the filters. If there'd been an ashtray, she wanted to say, she would have used it.

"'n I get a smoke?" he asked.

"Oh, of course," she said. "Absolutely." She fished in her jeans pocket for the pack of Silk Cut and the disposable lighter and – as he had made no move to come to her – stood and walked to him. She took a cigarette and proffered it to him, but he reached to her other hand and took the whole pack from her.

Sophie told herself not to make a fuss, that she had a whole duty-free carton in her suitcase, but he simply stared for a moment at the pack's purple and white design – doubtless new and strange to him – and then handed it back to her, exchanging it for the single cigarette. She flicked the lighter into flame but he shook his head and placed the cigarette in the breast pocket of his oversize Tee. "Later," he said, and turned his attention back to the empty track.

Sophie, feeling that to simply go back to the bench would somehow be a sign of insecurity, or at least another act of unintentional disrespect, turned to Knicks, who had moved across to the edge of the platform to join them. "Train should be here any moment," she said.

"It's always late," he said.

"Oh," she said. "Do you take it often, then?"

Knicks shrugged, like he wasn't sure how to answer, as if 'often' needed defining more closely. "You got business in New York?" he said, and looked at her appraisingly. Not rudely. Like he was honestly trying to guess what the nature of such business might be.

"No," she said. "I'm going up for a friend's wedding."

"Your friend from New York?"

Sophie nodded and, hoping to claim some kinship-by-association, added more details. "Well, Connecticut originally. But she and Jonathan live in the Village."

Tee, still clutching his bag, was looking up and down the length of the platform. Almost systematically. The way a soldier might check the perimeter.

Knicks furrowed his brow at Sophie, puzzled. "The Village?" he said. "What d'you mean, 'the Village'? Like that movie?"

"Fuckers in red was the *shit*," threw in Tee with an almost embarrassed admiration, finally letting his bag down onto the platform. It settled with a clanking sound, as if it were full of metal.

"No," Sophie said. "Greenwich Village. You know."

Knicks's brow creased again, like he was trying to place it. Actually, he looked like he was *pretending* to try. As a kindness, perhaps. To humor her. "No," he finally said. "New York? You sure?"

Sophie nodded. "Manhattan," she said. "At the bottom."

There was a snort from Tee, too gestural to be clearly derision.

"Oh, Manhattan," said Knicks. "We from Queens."

"Yeah, but you must have *heard* of Greenwich Village, right?"

The boy's face stiffened into a cold stare. "I said no."

Good God, I hurt his feelings, Sophie thought. Made him feel ig-norant. His emotions are so . . . *instant.* Like an animal's. Oh, that's a nice observation, Sophie, she told herself. Why don't you share that with him, see how he responds?

Looking away to avoid his eyes, Sophie pretended to look down the length of track to see if the train was coming. She noticed the toe of Tee's sneaker was pinching the edge of his canvas bag to the floor as if he feared its escape.

Knicks broke his brief silence. "You got your ticket already?"

His voice was warmer again. Sophie looked back at him and smiled. "Yes," she said. "Have you?"

"Nah, I got to pay on the train," he said. "Thirty-five dollars."

His tone betrayed nothing more than a quiet respect for that kind of money.

"Uh-huh," said Sophie, who'd paid considerably more than that for her sleeper compartment but thought it perhaps best not to say so right at that moment.

"Yeah," said Knicks, nodding now with an air of sad resignation. "Problem is, I only got thirty." He looked at her.

"Oh," said Sophie.

"Yeah," he said. And, after a decent interval; "So I need another five dollars."

"I see," said Sophie, nodding like she agreed with his math.

Knicks looked at her, sidelong, and gave a slow shy smile. Not a hint of aggression in it, Sophie noticed. Almost sheepish, in fact. Like he'd been caught in a marginally embarrassing situation. "Think you could help me out?"

Sophie exhaled slowly. Okay. No biggie. Five dollars, for Christ's sake. And he wasn't demanding, wasn't threatening, was just asking. He might even be telling the truth.

Grateful that she'd thought to put some ready-money in the back pocket of her jeans – God forbid she started rooting around in her purse with its stack of ready-for-Fifth-Avenue mad money – she casually pulled out the little wad of notes and peeled off a five.

"Sure," she said, handing it to him with a proudly untrembling hand. "Couldn't see you get thrown off the train. Not after we've been waiting together. Keeping each other company and, you know, chatting and everything." She smiled and tried to keep her voice casual – like she was utterly unaware of any subtext in what was going on. Just one new friend helping out another. Like normal people. Happens everyday. Nothing weird or threatening here.

Knicks nodded his thanks, looked expressionlessly at the bill and thrust it into his own pocket.

"Yeah," he said, nodding again. And then added – still with a tone of shy regret – "I really need the whole thirty-five."

Her reason told Sophie that she could say no, that he was just trying it on, testing her limits, that a firm but friendly *I'm sorry, I just can't do that* would end it all. But her body was telling her reason that it was an idiot. Her body felt differently about the situation. Her body – weak legs, racing heart, dry mouth – was saying that they were in trouble and that it was only going to escalate.

And then Tee spoke up.

"I need it, too," he said.

And there was nothing sheepish about his grin. It was lupine and delighted.

He looked ready to say more, ready perhaps to give an eager verbal preview of what else might happen in Sophie's life before the train arrived, but he suddenly snapped his head to the side.

His ears were sharper than those of Sophie or Knicks, but after a confused moment they heard it too.

Tap-tap-tap.

Someone was coming down the stone steps.

Sophie looked up, hoping to see a uniform, preferably that of a cop though she'd settle for that of a Station Guard, a Ticket Inspector, anybody that could even pretend to any kind of authority. But the person coming down, his walking cane tap-tap-tapping on the concrete, was just an old man in a regular suit.

All three of them watched as he walked across the platform toward the bench where Sophie had been sitting. His skin, darker than that of either of the boys, was smooth and unlined, but his hair was sparse and graying and – proving the cane was no affectation, despite the splendor of its silver headpiece – there was a stiffness and slowness to his movements. Even so, he moved with a memory of grace, as if conjuring the ghost of an elegant younger self that he had temporarily misplaced.

He himself cast nothing more than what appeared to be a casual glance at his fellow travelers. But as soon as he settled himself, both hands resting on the top of his cane, he called over to Sophie.

"Young lady," he said. "Would you care to keep an old man company?"

Sophie felt a warm rush of gratitude. She knew better than to look at either of the two boys, knew that it would look like she was asking permission. She crossed immediately back to the bench and sat beside the newcomer.

"Hello," she said, "I'm Sophie," and tried to keep her voice steady, to show neither relief nor fear.

The boys were approaching the bench now, too, but the old man kept his eyes on her and spoke as calmly as if they'd just been introduced at an afternoon tea party. "I'm very pleased to meet you, Sophie," he said, taking one hand from his cane to shake hers. "My name is Tillman. I'm eighty years old, but your beauty makes me feel like a boy of sixty-three." He winked at her. He had a pencil-mustache that was less gray than his hair and a pocket handkerchief in his jacket that matched his tie.

Only as the boys arrived at the bench did he look up. He nodded courteously to them. "The lady's name is Sophie, gentlemen," he said. "From the Greek *sophia*, which means wisdom. Isn't that just a lovely name for parents to give to their child? Like a promise and a hope that she will one day grow into the meaning of her name."

The two boys exchanged a glance, and Tee, looking back at Tillman, gave a tight little grin, half amused and half contemptuous, like whatever the old man had said was just so much static.

"You a preacher?" asked Knicks, again with that air of open-hearted enquiry, like he was interested in the world and not just what he could get from it.

Tillman chuckled. "No, indeed," he said.

"Ain't no damn preacher, fool," said Tee. "Check out the clothes. Grampa's a pimp. Tryin' to turn this bitch out."

The shorter boy snickered and flicked a hand-sign like his friend had scored a point.

"Not hardly, young man," Tillman said, refusing to be offended. "I was a singer. Still am, I suppose. Though it's a long time since I seen the other fellas and it never felt right singing without them."

"You was in a band?" Tee said. "*What* band?" It was an expression of unfriendly disbelief rather than interest.

"We called ourselves The Invisible Kings," Tillman said, and there was a fifty-year-old pride in his voice as he said the name, as if he could hear somewhere the ghostly echo of ancient applause.

"Like, Gospel?" said Knicks.

"Not strictly, son, no. Though we were a vocal group."

"Doo-wop?" said Sophie. "Like The Orioles?" She'd heard their version of *Crying in the Chapel* at her grandmother's house many years ago.

The old man turned to face her and treated her to a smile that revealed one single bright gold crown among the nicotined yellow of his teeth.

"Ah," he said. "I see we have a scholar among us."

"Did you make any *records*?" she said, partly to try and keep the conversation on this topic rather than anything else the boys might have in mind and partly out of what would have been in any other circumstance an intrigued delight. But before Tillman could answer, Tee cut in.

"Enough!" he said. "Go take a walk, old man. We was in the middle of something." And he let his gaze shift to Sophie.

Tillman nodded understandingly.

"I'm sure you were," he said. "Probably always in the middle of something. Who can blame you? Couple young lions like you, it's just your nature." His tone was respectful, a quarter-notch *too* respectful, and Sophie realized with a sinking heart that beneath his gravity and charm he was almost as afraid as she. Nevertheless, he put a hand out slowly and, laying it gently on Tee's hand, the hand that was gripping the hold-all, said in a firmer voice: "But I'm asking you to rise above your nature."

"Mind your goddam business," the boy said, and shook his hand angrily free. Again, that heavy metallic clatter from within the bag.

Tillman glanced briefly at the bag and then up at its owner. "No waiting period in this state, is there?" he said.

Tee's other hand flew out and slapped Tillman hard across the mouth. "Shut the fuck up!" he said.

"Don't hurt him!" Sophie shouted. She started to stand, but Knicks pushed her back effortlessly onto the bench and then stepped back, bouncing with nervous energy from foot to foot, eyes flicking to his friend like an athlete awaiting his coach's instruction. Only as it fled from her did Sophie understand that she'd been holding a tiny hope that he may have proved a moderating influence on his friend.

Tillman straightened up from the slap slowly and painfully, his tongue exploring his teeth and the inside of his cheek. His voice was still very calm. "Young man," he said to Tee, "you are frightening me."

"First smart thing you said. Stay frightened."

Tillman nodded in acquiescence. "I will," he said. "If you'll do something for me."

He raised a placatory hand before Tee could remind him who was boss. "It'll cost you nothing but time, I promise. Will you let me tell you a story?"

"'the fuck?" said Knicks.

"Train's always late," said Tillman. "Where's the harm?" He looked at each young man in turn. Humble. Unthreatening.

Tee looked at him steadily for a moment. He reached into his breast pocket and put the cigarette in his mouth. He thrust his hand at Sophie and snapped his fingers. She pulled out her lighter and handed it to him. He lit the cigarette, pocketed the lighter, and looked at Tillman. "You got this long," he said, gesturing with the cigarette.

Tillman nodded, like that was perfectly reasonable. "This story," he said, "is what the Jewish folk call apocryphal. That means it wasn't one of the stories that they put in their books. But it doesn't mean it didn't happen.

"Now, back in the day there was a mighty ruler of a mighty kingdom. Could've been Babylon, could've been Assyria. Tell the truth, it's slipped my mind and it don't count for shit anyway. You'll pardon my rough language, Miss Sophie, but a story's got to have some grit to it or it ain't worth the telling. What counts was that this mighty ruler, despite his armies and his empires, despite his palaces and his slaves, couldn't rule the heart of his own Queen.

"The Queen, you see, was all moon-eyed over a fine-looking young

Israelite priest who'd been given over to this pagan kingdom in return for . . . I don't know, seven years of good crops or some such . . . always something like that going on, right? Anyway, this priest was an upright fellow, by all accounts, and did nothing to encourage her but that didn't matter to the King. It just twisted him up inside to see the way she'd look at the fellow and so one day, when he couldn't take it any more, he had a couple of his boys take their daggers and throw themselves a party on the priest's beautiful face. In some versions, I'm sorry to say, he also had his Queen's eyes put out, but we don't have to believe that if we don't want to.

"Point is, the King wasn't done with the priest. He thought it would wrap everything up nicely if he put him in a lion pit. 'Course, this was back when every self-respecting mighty ruler had to have himself a lion-pit and our man was no exception. He had lions, yessir. Kept them close at hand for whenever opportunity presented itself for some entertainment.

"Funny thing is, the lions weren't interested at first. The Priest just stood there in the pit – King and his posse watching from the good seats – and was ignored by the lions. Maybe they'd eaten somebody else earlier that day. Maybe they was just enjoying the sun, stretching out there in the warmth, feeling all good and lionish, like nothing in the world's going to fuck with them, they being kings of the goddam jungle and all. So they hardly even looked at the priest, just left him alone to stand there, thinking on the ruin of his face.

"But you know how it is with lions.

"Eventually, they're going to think, *Hey, wait a minute* – and they'll take a little sniff – *here's something warm and just full of blood and meat. Seems we'd hardly be fit to call ourselves lions if we don't kill ourselves some of that.*

"And that's what happened. They stood up – maybe they roared a little to let him know what was coming – and then they charged."

Tillman stopped talking. He cleared his throat and tapped his cane once or twice on the concrete of the platform.

"Pfft," said Tee, whose cigarette was nearly done. Knicks simply stared at Tillman, his brow back in its furrow, like he thought he was having a trick played on him that he didn't yet understand.

"Wait," said Sophie. "What happened?"

166

"Well, accounts differ," Tillman said. "In some versions, the lions ate the priest and life went on, as it does. And I guess the moral would be *Sometimes you're just in the wrong damn place at the wrong damn time.*" He paused. "But what kind of ending is that? No, the real story – and listen closely now, boys, because you'll like this – is that that priest was just about done with this King and all his shit, and so he stood his ground before those charging lions, and he opened his mouth, and he roared right back at them. But what came out of his mouth – and who knows why? Maybe because this priest was a good man in the eyes of his Lord, maybe because his Lord was just about done with this King and all his shit, too – what came out of his mouth was a single sublime note. Loud as thunder. Sweet as honey. High and pure and holy. And deadly as the wrath of God.

"And this note – which, let's call a spade a spade here, boys, was to all intents and purposes the very voice of Jehovah himself – it slew the lions, it slew the King, it slew every motherfucker within three square miles of that damn lion pit, and it laid waste to the palaces of the pagan."

Tillman sighed, deflating himself from the declamatory style to which he had climbed. But he raised a finger to stop anybody else from talking, for he wasn't quite done.

"And that would be the end of the story," he said, his voice now calm and gentle again, "except that, despite all that slaying and laying waste, despite all that righteous devastation, there was one surviving witness – always is, right, else how do we hear the stories? – and this witness carried the memory of that killing note with him and he taught it to himself till he had it almost right. Never as good as the original, mind, never as pure or powerful. But good enough for government work, if you catch my drift. And before his days on earth were done, he taught it to one other, who taught it to one other, who taught it to one other, who . . . well, you get the point. You've heard stories like this before.

"I'm pretty much done, boys, and I see that that cigarette is finished. So I'll just say this; I am a long-lived and well-traveled man and I have learned many interesting things in my time in this world. I thank you for your attention and patience. And now you must do whatever it is you will do."

Sophie sat there, silent, utterly unsure of how to respond.

Not so Tee. He knew a challenge when he heard one. "Bullshit," he said.

"Maybe," said Tillman. And locked his unblinking eyes on those of the boy.

Sophie wanted to tell Tillman to stop. Could he not see the rage building in Tee? The clenched teeth and blazing eyes? She looked to Knicks, hoping there'd be some way to defuse this. But he was committed to the moment too, his smile back, eager for something interesting to happen, looking up and down the platform to confirm there would be no witnesses.

Tee yanked open the zipper of his bag and plunged his hand inside, never once taking his eyes off Tillman's.

"Fuck you," he said, and leveled the gun at the old man's face.

Tillman opened his mouth.

From what Sophie heard, before the gun exploded and she fainted, the note was high and pure, just like he'd said.

❀

Something was whistling.

There was another sound too, like mighty engines settling and creaking into stillness.

Sophie opened her eyes to find herself staring at the long black train completely filling the length of the track in front of her.

The engines and wheels continued their decompression, filling the night with a sound like a long melancholy breath.

"The sigh of midnight trains in empty stations," said Tillman's voice.

Still blinking herself awake, still not sure where exactly she was or what exactly had happened, Sophie turned to see that the old man was still beside her on the bench.

He'd sounded as if he was quoting something, and she saw that he was looking at her expectantly. "No?" he said, after a few moments.

Sophie smiled and shook her head.

"*These Foolish Things*," he said. "Lovely song. We cut a version of it back in nineteen and sixty-one, but I'm sorry to say it never got released."

"Title sounds familiar," Sophie said.

"Lyric was by one of your people," Tillman said. "English, I mean. Holt Marvell, he called himself. Real name was Erich Maschwitz. A true poet of the bitter-sweet."

Sophie looked around. "Where are --?"

"Oh, they're already on board," he said, interrupting her and standing.

The train was long and black and lightless and had no name or logo. Sophie looked at it, puzzled and a little disconcerted, but made to stand also, her hand reaching for the handle of her suitcase.

The old man's hand patted her forearm gently in a staying motion.

"No, little sweetness," he said. "This train doesn't stop where you're going."

He walked toward the train, toward the door that creaked open for him. Just before stepping inside, he turned to look back at her one last time.

"*Crescent* be along soon as we pull out of here, don't you worry," he said, and smiled in farewell, the glint of that single gold tooth catching the starlight.

Sophie raised her hand in a motionless wave, tried to smile, tried to speak. Couldn't.

But she blew him a kiss that she knew he saw before the door shut over him, the clang of its closing all but lost in the deep thunder of the black wheels of the night train beginning to turn.

DANCING LIKE WE'RE DUMB

Punk in the back seat didn't look so tough, but the jittery eagerness with which he pressed the barrel of his Ruger against the back of my headrest talked me out of giving him the kind of shit I'd normally enjoy throwing his way.

I was in the front passenger seat—annoying to begin with because it was my fucking car—and Jumpy McHandgun back there was the monkey to Cody Garrity's organ-grinder. Cody was driving. Not driving well, it has to be said, but certainly letting the State know what it could do with its posted speed limits.

I'd had the pleasure of their acquaintance a mere four minutes or so and I knew Cody's name only because he was the kind of tool that liked to introduce himself when he was carjacking you.

"Hi, I'm Cody Garrity," he'd said. "Slide over." His Smith & Wesson .38 had been on display for me but held flat against his stomach to avoid alarming anyone else in the Albertson's parking lot.

I got to give them props for the smoothness of their work. Cody'd ambled schlub-like between the spots like some harmless stoner who'd forgotten where he'd parked, while his neck-tattooed catamite kept himself completely out of sight until Cody'd already got the drop on me.

I'd only been driving Ilsa, She-wolf of the SS, for a month or so and, while she may have been merely an entry-level Mercedes, she was still a Mercedes so I should have been paying more fucking attention. It's true that it was four o'clock in the afternoon of another perfect LA day and that seven years of driving third-hand Detroit may well have dulled my douchebags-who-want-your-stuff antenna but I'm not going to make excuses. I'd been sitting there checking my mental shopping list with the driver door wide open like some middle-class moron who thinks crime only happens to other people, so I've got no-one to blame but Mrs. Donnelly's youngest.

Cody, jumping lights and ignoring stop signs, was tearing down Griffith Park Boulevard now, pushing Ilsa like he had her on a Nascar track instead of a residential street, and her engine was purring pleasurably in response to his aggression. Little kraut slut.

"What you got on your pre-sets?" Cody asked, but was already stabbing at the radio's buttons. The speakers burst into life and the godlike genius known to an undeserving world as Ke$ha told us she had Jesus on her necklace.

Cody gave me a superior look. "Top forty," he said, like I needed my channels explaining. His tone was derisive, and the epsilon in back snorted in agreement. Their disdain didn't surprise me. What did surprise me—confused me, in fact—was that I was still in the damn car. I don't know if Cody and his chimp had ever read *Carjacking for Dummies* but if they had I'm pretty sure they'd have learned that the place to say goodbye to their new vehicle's previous owner was back at the point of purchase.

It's never a good idea to point out examples of their own stupidity to boys who like to play with guns but I needed to let them know that, now that they had the car and all, it was time that they thought about ditching the unwanted baggage. I turned to look at Cody—always smarter to talk to the less-amped one—and pointed ahead to the next intersection.

"You could drop me at the corner of Hyperion," I said, calm as a tween on Ritalin. "I can pick up a slice at Hard Times and—"

"Hey, lesbo at frontseat dot com," his partner interrupted. "Shut the fuck up."

Well, that was alarming. Not a single Melissa CD or Ellen bio in sight and me in my usual show-the-boys-what-they're-missing drag, but still Antsy Von Rugerstein—who I'm guessing wasn't the brightest bitch in his pack—had me down as a friend of Radclyffe Hall. Which meant he had to have come armed with prior knowledge. Which meant he and his alpha hadn't been targeting Ilsa at all. They'd been targeting me.

Huh. And the day'd started off so quiet.

Started off nice, in fact. Coffee at my place with a pretty girl.

Anna was almost eighteen, exclusively and unfortunately hetero, and was part of a grrl power trio called The Butchered Barbies. Anna had two jobs in the band—to play bass and to look hot—and was good at one of them. The Barbies—who were almost big in what remained of the Silverlake scene—were all buzzsaw guitar and Jenny Rotten snarls, like the last thirty years had never happened. I'd tried to point out to Anna on more than one occasion that their whole schtick was as charmingly antiquarian as crinolines and afternoon tea but she wasn't having it. Fucking kids. No telling them.

Anyway, Anna had come calling this morning because she'd misplaced a piece of vinyl that meant a lot to her and was flirting with the idea that it had been stolen and wanted me to flirt with the idea of making it my next case.

Next case. Jesus Christ. Truth is I feel weird even talking about cases. I mean, with my impressive juvenile resumé of drug-running and related criminal activities, it wasn't like the State was going to fucking *license* me any time soon. And, besides, most of the people who came to me with their little problems weren't the sort of people who were likely to want the authorities anywhere within sniffing distance of their own shit. Nevertheless, for the last eighteen months or so the Donnelly larder had been stocked pretty exclusively by the proceeds of a series of adventures in private investigation, so turns out—licensed or not—I'd sashayed my way into becoming Nancy Drew for the meh generation.

"It was that guy," Anna said. "I'm pretty sure. Have you got any more coffee?" She looked around my kitchenette with a hopeful expression like the coffee could perhaps be somewhere other than the auto-drip's empty pitcher and waggled her mug on the counter-top like she might tempt it out of hiding.

"I'll make some," I said, getting up. "What guy?"

"The *guy*," she said, giving me a look like what the fuck was wrong with me not keeping up with her tweets.

"Remind me," I said, walking to the machine and swapping out the used filter.

"Took a stranger home after a gig," she said. "Fucked him. Gone when I woke up. No name, no number. One of my 45s was missing."

Come on. Of course that's not what she said. What she *said* took the entire brew-cycle but I've done you the courtesy of editing out the how-she-felt and the what-she-wore and the how-he-seemed-nice and the Emma's-cool-but-she-can-be-so-jealous and all the rest of her Proustian-level-of-detail shit. Trust me, you owe me big.

I'd press her later for more clues to the identity of the gentle and sensitive young poet with whom she'd shared those brief idyllic moments, but first I wanted to know if what might have been stolen was something actually worth stealing. I asked her the name of the missing single.

"You probably haven't heard of it, Kitty," she said gently—you know, me being twenty-five and such a fucking square and all. "It's called 'The Devil Rides Shotgun', by Guest Eagleton."

Bless her. Everything's new to seventeen year olds, even history. The record in question was certainly a rarity but the story behind it was hardly obscure. They even made a bad TV movie about it in the early 80s, something I resisted telling Anna for fear it would break her hip little heart. Rockabilly legend Eagleton—not a legend at the time, of course, just another redneck punk lucky enough to be making a third single because his second had crossed over from the regional charts to the lower reaches of the Billboard Hot 100—recorded 'The Devil Rides Shotgun' in 1957. By all accounts, the recording itself went fine—single hanging mike, three piece band, two takes and off to the cathouse, those were the days—but between the day of the recording and the release of the single Guest finally got around to reading his contract.

Discovering that the label's owner—a scurrilous one, imagine that—had put himself up as co-writer of the song, young Guest, still fresh from the Kentucky hills and not one to wait for lawyers when there's a sawn-off handy, broke into the record plant to personally stop the pressing of the 45.

Here's the part of the story where fact shades into legend. It's a fact Guest was shot by the first cop on the scene. It's a fact that he fell from the gantry into the production line below. I don't know for a fact he was dead before his face landed in the hot wax vat, but I sure hope so. It's a fact that twenty-seven copies of the 45 were pressed before they could shut the line down. And the legend, of course, is that each of those twenty-seven copies contains microscopic remnants of their late creator because the flesh that was stripped from his skull by the molten vinyl was swirled away with it and stamped into the records themselves. You can believe it if you like. Snopes gives it a cautious "hasn't actually been disproved" kind of rating.

Anyway, the final fact is that—whether the story of their extra ingredient was true or not—those copies of the single, though never officially released, have become Grail-like to serious vinyl junkies over the years. Springsteen paid nearly twenty grand for his copy back in his glory days, the nerd from Coldplay almost twice as much at a Sotheby's auction three years ago. Anna got hers as a gift. Like I said, pretty girl.

It wasn't even lunchtime before I was cooling my heels in the lobby of a mid-level talent agency on Beverly waiting to see the douche who'd picked Anna up and ask him nicely for the return of her property.

Here's the thing about detecting that my more invested-in-the-myth colleagues don't want you to know: Like every other job, it's really easy except for those rare but annoying times when it's not. This thing of Anna's took me one phone call to a barman I knew at the club where the Barbies had played, another to a customer he knew who'd spent time talking to the aforementioned douche, and a quick internet search of employment records.

I'd given my name to the pretty young man at the reception desk and told him I needed to see Andy Velasco on a personal matter of some urgency. He'd told me he'd do what he could but that Mr. Velasco was very busy and I'd bit my tongue and sat down to wait. But by the time I'd read *Variety* from cover to cover I figured I'd waited long enough and, in the next brief gap in the endless phone calls the receptionist was fielding, walked back over to his desk and said, "Where's his office?"

The receptionist pulled a face. "I'm going to need you to sit down and be patient."

"When?" I asked him.

"Excuse me?"

"When are you going to need me to do that?"

He hesitated, because—how the hell would he know—maybe I actually was that stupid.

"Now," he said, with that weary politeness that's supposed to let you know you're dealing with a trained professional.

"Now?" I said. "So what's with all the 'I'm going to' crap? Present tense. Future tense. They're different for a reason." Poor bastard. Wasn't like he was the only idiot to talk that way but, you know, millionth customer gets the confetti and the coupon-book. Luck of the draw.

"I need you to sit down," he said. "Now." Giving it his best firm and authoritative, just like the manual must've told him. Adorable.

"Well, I need Scarlett Johansson and a fistful of Rohypnol," I said. "So that's two of us that are shit out of luck."

"*I* have no problem with calling the Police," he said.

"Me neither," I said. "But I can guarantee you your Mr. Velasco would." He came up short on the snappy comeback front so I pressed on. "Tell him I've got a pitch for him. Re-imagining of an old classic. *Statutory Rape and the Single Rockchick*. Pretty sure he'll want to hear it."

Five minutes later, I was driving the single back to Anna's place in Echo Park.

And five hours later, after a breakneck jaunt up and around the curves of Mulholland, I was about to be ushered in to a mansion on a hill by my new friend Cody Garrity.

176

His little helper had clambered into Ilsa's driver seat when Cody and I'd got out and, as he slipped her back into drive and started out of the courtyard roundabout, he dropped the window, grinned at me, and pantomimed a shot to my head. Charm. It's just something you're born with.

I returned the smile and nodded. "Catch you later," I said.

He didn't much care for the way I'd said it, I guess, because he slammed back into park like he was ready to get out and teach the bitch some manners.

"Scott..." Cody said. Not much spin on it, but apparently enough to get the little tyke back in his cage. He drove off, and I watched him exit through the big wrought-iron gates. Neck tattoo, five foot six, name of Scott. Should be enough. It's always nice to have something to look forward to.

"Long walk back," I said to Cody. "But at least it's downhill."

"I got a ride," he said, cocking his head in the direction of a late model Cadillac parked outside a separate Carriage House. "And you're not going to need one."

"Ominous," I said. "I'm all a-tremble."

"Comedienne," he said—yeah, four syllables, gender-specific and everything, who knew?—and waved me toward the front door of the main house with his gun.

Quite a place. And it sure as hell didn't belong to Cody. Nor did it belong to a pissant junior agent like Andy Velasco—to whom I should perhaps have paid more attention when he told me that he was just a middleman and that his client was not going to be happy—because this place was money. Real money.

The three rooms and a hallway we walked through to get where we were going were high-end SoCal class. Impressive and imposing but nothing you haven't seen in the glossies. The room we ended up in though was something quite different. Black marble and red lacquer and display cases full of books, artifacts, and impedimenta of a very specific nature.

Shit.

Magic. I *hate* magic.

❀

LA's just full of Satanists. Always has been. I don't know if it's some kind of yin yang natural balance thing—all that sun, surf, and simplicity needing to be contrasted by some really dark shit—but it certainly seems that way. Into every Brian Wilson's life, a little Charlie Manson must fall.

Most of the Golden State's followers of the left hand path are of course idiot dilettantes chasing tail and money but every now and then something real fucking ugly breaks surface. Something that knows what it's doing.

It was hard to think of the seventy year old guy who'd been waiting for us in the room as someone who knew what he was doing, though, at least when it came to raising demons and the like. Getting into pickles with pretty sitcom moms, sure, or raising exasperated eyebrows at the antics of adorable juvenile leads maybe. I recognized him immediately, and you would've too. I doubt you could watch four hours of *TV Land* without seeing him at least twice. Never had his own show but from the late 60s through the mid 80s he was very solidly employed. You'd have as hard a time as I did remembering the name—Frankie Metcalfe, I eventually recalled—but you'd know the face in a heartbeat. Still worked now and then; he did one of those standard Emmy-baiting lovable-old-curmudgeon-with-Cancer bits on *Grey's Anatomy* couple of seasons back.

"Really?" I said. "*There Goes the Neighborhood* residuals can get you a place like this?"

"Hardly," he said. "Bequest from an acolyte. So you're the interfering little cunt who decided she'd piss on my parade?"

Whoa. Quite a mouth. And from *this* guy? It was like hearing Howie Cunningham tell you to go fuck your mother.

"Why didn't you just make Anna an offer?" I said. "You probably could have got the damn single for less than a month's worth of property tax."

"Not an option," he said. "The ritual has its rules."

Christ almighty. Always with the rules and rituals, these dickheads. Flying the flag for transgression and the dark arts, but as prissy about it as a chapter of the fucking DAR.

"Esoteric as all get out, I'm sure," I said. "Can I give you a piece of friendly advice? Payback for all those hours of televisual pleasure? If you have a gun handy, you might want to get it now."

"Because?"

"Because sometime in the next five or ten minutes I'm going to re-lieve Cody of his and blow the top of his fucking head off and I'd hate for you to be caught at a disadvantage."

Cody bristled at that—big fucking deal, I've been bristled at before—but Frankie laughed. I think he was starting to like me.

I wondered why he'd sent his boys to grab me instead of just having them snatch the single again, and asked him.

"Your friend was apparently so moved by its safe return that she's keeping it about her person," Frankie said. "Which wouldn't be a problem, but her group is currently traveling." He looked to Cody for details.

"They got a gig in Bakersfield tonight," Cody said.

"Bakersfield?" I said. "Seriously, the Barbies? Buck Owens must be turning over in his grave."

Frankie ignored the sidebar. "So, no *memento mori* of the unfor-tunate Mister Eagleton," he said. "Still, not to worry. We've got you instead."

"I'm a girl of many talents," I said. "But singing isn't one of them."

"Then how lucky we are that all you'll be required to do is die. Let's move the party down below, shall we?"

We were on the ground floor, in case I haven't made that clear. "Down below," I said. "That's quite unusual for Los Angeles." Look at *me*, being all up on my building codes and shit.

"What is?" Frankie asked.

"Having a basement."

"Oh, I don't have a basement," he said.

He was right. He didn't have a basement. What he had was a cav-ern. I'd have made the requisite Bruce Wayne jokes except the sight of it didn't really inspire humor.

It was huge, for starters, like the hill beneath his house and those of his neighbors lower down on the slope was absolutely hollow. And the hollowness was new. I don't mean man-made new—there'd been no excavation here, at least not by natural means—but alarmingly, preternaturally new, like the hill was eating itself hollow in preparation for something. The hill was being rewritten, I thought, though I'd have preferred not to. The cavern walls weren't of rock, but of whatever primordial clay once hardened into rock. They were pale brown, and wet. Oozing wet, like the whole thing was sweating feverishly. The floor was the same, sucking at our feet with every step. That I could handle. It was the breathing that freaked me the fuck out.

It was slow and labored and, apart from being a hundred times as loud and coming from everywhere at once, sounded like the melancholy and heartbreaking sound of someone on their deathbed. But this wasn't the sound of something dying. It was the sound of something being born. And it bothered me. A lot.

But not as much as it bothered Cody.

We'd descended by rope ladder from a trapdoor in Frankie's souvenir shop—the descent being, too bad for me, textbook smart; guy with gun first, unarmed chick second, creepy old guy third—and ever since we'd got here, Cody'd evidenced increasing signs of having got himself into something that wasn't what he thought he'd signed up for.

Yeah, well too damn bad, Gangsta.

Once his awestruck and unhappy glances at his surroundings started to occupy more of each of his last minutes on earth than his glances at me did, I figured it was time to put him out of his misery.

I couldn't even feel smug about it, guy was so out of his comfort zone. A slight hesitation, as if I was mesmerized by one of the clay-like excrescences that bloomed from the dripping walls like attempts at imitating local flora, a misdirecting glance back behind him, and then a well-placed heel and elbow, and he was on his knees, gasping for breath, and his gun was in my unforgiving hand.

"Say goodnight, Cody," I said, and put one through the centre of his forehead.

I was swinging back towards where I'd last seen Frankie when I heard the click of his safety and felt his barrel at the back of my neck. Cargo pants don't look that great on guys his age but they do have a lot of pocket space.

"Leave it with him," Frankie said, and I dropped the .38 on Cody's dead chest.

"Watch," Frankie said, trying for dispassionate but failing to completely mask the fascination and excitement.

So I watched. Partly because information is power, and partly because Mom always told me it's a bad idea to piss off a crazy old fucker with a gun.

The blood jetting out of Cody's shattered skull was being sucked into the liquid sheen of the clay like mother's milk into the mouth of a greedy newborn. And it was a two-way street. Cody's flesh was invaded by the fecal brown of the mud he'd died on until, inside of a minute, he looked like something somebody'd molded from the wet and alien earth itself.

So much for any lingering hope that this could all be explained away by sedimentary settlement.

"It accepts the offering," Frankie said, more out there by the fucking minute. "But don't entertain any hope that this can replace your own sacrifice. There was no gravitas here. No ceremony. The unfortunate news for you is that your death needs to be both slow and somewhat spectacular."

Fuck me. With the exception of his charming opening gambit with the C word back in his trophy room, everything this guy said sounded like he'd lifted it from his back catalogue of crappy scripts. Case in point, his subsequent lurid description of what I had to look forward to before the day was much older.

"I'm going to blah blah blah. Blah blah blah, Kitty, blah blah blah." On and fucking on. Use your imagination. I assure you it's at least as good as his.

"That how you get it up?" I said, when he was finally done. "Telling girls what you're going to do to them?"

"No, Ms. Donnelly," he said. "I get it up watching people's eyes turn glassy with dread as they feel all hope of escape disappear." TV's Frankie Metcalfe, Ladies and Gentlemen. A real fucking sweetheart. "Now, let's move on to the central chamber."

We moved ahead through a curving anterior walkway. Only then, within its lower ceiling and narrower walls, did I pause to wonder where the hell the light was coming from. But it was a meaningless question. I could see perfectly well. And I had no idea how or why.

Another of those misshapen flowers was growing from the weeping wall to our left. This one was vanguard minded, attempting an impression of color, its stalk and leaves blood red, its petals an eerie and bilious yellow. Frankie's left hand plucked it from the wall with a flourish.

"Here," he said, shaking some of its slime from his fingers and flinging it at me. "Pretend it's Prom Night."

"Thanks," I said, catching it and pretending to sniff it before holding it to my wrist like a corsage. "Every time I smell it, I'll think of you."

He gave me a look that told me he was smart enough to know I'd stolen the line but not sharp enough to remember from whom—let me save you the Google; it was my fellow Irish deviant, Oscar Wilde—and then, all done with our little time-out flirtation, waved me ahead impatiently, waggling the gun like a signaling device.

"Got it," he said. "You're un-fucking-flappable. Now get moving, or I'll drag you there by the short and curlies."

Sad old bastard. Like anybody has pubic hair anymore. I dropped the nasty little flower—wet and rubbery and pulsing unpleasantly like it hadn't yet decided its final shape—and moved ahead of him, conceding reluctantly to myself as I walked on that things were not looking good for our plucky girl detective. Fact, I could feel *The Adventure of the Hollow Hill* lobbying to give itself a real fucking downer of an ending as I stepped out from the walkway into what he'd called the central chamber. There was a bubbling quicksand-like pool at its heart, surrounded by several ill-defined shapes that put me in mind of the grotesque statue that Cody's body had become. More formal offerings, I thought. The place was a compost heap, a mulch pit, and Frankie's ode to its insane splendor confirmed as much.

"You've doubtless seen all that pentagram and puff of smoke nonsense in the movies," he said. "But the truth is it takes time and effort to actually effect a materialization. The ground must be prepared. I've been seeding it for years, Kitty. Seeding it with frozen pain, with artifacts that contain the captured essence of human suffering. I've brought such treasures here. The skulls of slaughtered children, a letter to the media that one of our most celebrated serial killers wrote in the blood of a victim, a copy of the *De Vermis Mysteriis* bound in human skin. 'The Devil Rides Shotgun' would have been a beautiful addition, but alas…"

He let his voice trail off theatrically. Prime fucking ham.

I'd have asked him the obvious question—*why the hell are you doing this?*—but I knew there was no point. He wouldn't have an answer because he wasn't really here anymore. He was as hollow as his hill, and just as much in the process of transformation. Whatever the human motivations that had kicked him off—curiosity, excitement, thrill of the forbidden, whatever—he was now merely a vessel of the Other's desire to manifest itself. He had nothing to do with it. He was long gone. Whatever was blossoming in his cavern had eaten Frankie Metcalfe from the inside too.

So why leave the crust?

He was staring at the bubbling pool at the heart of it all and, for a second or two, hardly paying attention to me. I'd think later that perhaps either outcome was equally acceptable to what was left of the man he used to be, but I wouldn't think about it much because it allowed for too much human ambiguity in the monster he'd become. I sure as shit didn't think about it in the moment. I was younger and faster and all his meditative pause in the proceedings meant to me was this: Forget the gun, close the gap, get one hand on his skull and the other on his chin, and snap his wretched ancient neck like a fucking twig.

I'd have run anyway, but the terrifying re-ossification of the whole cavern lent my legs a whole new level of motivation. Killing Frankie had been like flipping a power-down switch on whatever he'd been ushering in to our world. It made sense, I suppose. Any other death down here—like, you know, mine—would have been just more mulch on the shit-pile of its becoming, but the death of its possessed summoner threw everything into reverse. Whatever had been coming was now retreating and the hill was reclaiming its solidity. Reclaiming it, thank fuck, not quite as fast as I reclaimed the rope ladder and clambered my way back up into the house.

By the time I let myself out of the front door and headed for the Cadillac, the sun was just starting to set. California perfect. Orange and blue and purple and beautiful.

But I wasn't really thinking about that. I was thinking about this:

Neck tattoo, five foot six, name of Scott.

Catch you later.

FRUMPY LITTLE
BEAT GIRL

"They don't make hats like that anymore," says Mr. Slater.

Jesus. Five minutes in and first thing out of his mouth. Bethany looks up from her book and through the windshield to see what the hell he's talking about.

There's a pedestrian, a Hispanic guy, crossing in front of the Lexus. He's in no particular hurry about it, and he doesn't need to be. The light they're stuck at, the one at San Fernando and Brand, can take three minutes even in a good mood and, at eight-thirty in the morning, you can usually count on it being pissy.

"Sure they do," Bethany says, meaning the hat.

"No," Mr. Slater says, his head moving to watch the man reach the sidewalk and turn to wait, like them, for the northbound green. Bethany hears the pleasure, the admiration, in his voice. "They make things that *look* like it, maybe," he says. "But that's *period*."

He has a point. It's not only the grey fedora. The pedestrian—elderly but vigorous, his body lean and compact, face like leather but like, you know, *good* leather—is dressed in a subtly-pinstriped black suit that could be new or that could have been really well looked after for decades. There's a tight quarter-inch of white handkerchief showing above the suit's breast pocket, and the man wears opinionated shoes.

"Cool," Bethany says. "*Buena Vista Social Club.*"

"You think he's Cuban?" Mr. Slater asks, as if she was being literal. "I mean, like, not Mexican?"

Bethany, no idea, shrugs and smiles. The light changes and Mr. Slater—*you know, you really can start calling me David*, he's said more than once but she's been baby-sitting for him and his wife since she was fourteen and just can't get her head around it—moves through the intersection and takes one last look back at the guy. "Check him out," he says, happy and impressed. "It's 1958. And it's never not going to be."

Gay Michael's on with a customer when Bethany comes into the bookstore but he takes the time to cover the phone's mouthpiece and stare pointedly out the plate-glass window as Mr. Slater's Lexus pulls away into the Glendale traffic. He gives her an eyebrow. "Bethany Lake," he says, delighted. "You appalling little slut."

"My neighbor," she starts to tell him, ready to add that she'd needed a ride because her piece-of-shit Dodge is in the shop again but he's already back on the phone giving directions.

"Yes, Ma'am," he's saying, "*Michael & Michael.* On Brand. Between Wilson and California." Listens for a moment. "Of course. Consider it held. And it really is in lovely condition. The website pictures don't do it justice." Bethany watches him run his hand over the tooled leather binding of the book on the counter in front of him as if he can send the seductive feel of it down the line. It's an 1827 *Paradise Lost*, the famous one with the John Martin mezzotints. Bethany catches his eye, points to the curtained annex at the rear of the store, mimes a coffee-cup at her mouth.

She'd figured she'd have to brew a fresh pot but Fat Michael's already on it; three mugs waiting, OCD-ed into a handle-matching line atop a napkin that's folded in geometric precision. On a shelf above the coffee-maker, his iPod is nestled in its cradle-and-mini-speakers set-up and its random shuffle—which Bethany pretends is a radio station with the call-sign K-FMO, for 'Fat Michael's Oddities'—is playing *Jack the Ripper* by Screaming Lord Sutch. "*Is your name Mary Blood?*" his Lordship is currently screaming, albeit at low volume; Fat Michael would like to pipe K-FMO through to the store, but Gay Michael's foot is firmly down on that one. "What are we, fucking Wal-Mart?" is about as far as the conversation ever gets.

"He's really got a bite on that Milton?" Bethany says, knowing the boys have been asking high four figures. The coffee-maker pings.

"Some sit-com star's trophy wife," Fat Michael says, filling Bethany's mug first and handing it to her, no milk no sugar, just right. "She's shopping for his birthday. You know, like he can read."

"None of your customers read, Michael," she says. "They *collect*."

"Hmph," he says, because he doesn't like to be reminded, and then, as the next selection comes up on K-FMO, "Oh, listen. It's your song."

It so is *not* her song. It's a bad novelty record called *Kinky Boots* about how everybody's wearing, you know, kinky boots. The only boots Bethany owns are a pair of Doc Martens but it wasn't footwear that had made the boys declare it her song. Couple of months earlier, Gay Michael, bored on a customerless afternoon, had treated her to an appraising look as she was leaning on the counter reading.

"Look at you," he'd said. "With your jean jacket and your ironic T-shirts." The one she'd been wearing that day had read *Talk Nerdy to Me*. "With your Aimee Bender paperbacks and your rah-rah skirts and leggings. You know what you are, Bethany? You're a frumpy little beat girl."

Fat Michael had clapped his hands in delight. Sometimes Bethany wondered which of the partners was actually the gay one. "*Sweet girls, Street girls, Frumpy little beat girls,*" he'd recited, just in case Bethany had missed the reference to the stupid song's lyrics. She couldn't be mad at either of them—it was all so obviously coming from a place of affection—but, you know, Jesus Christ. Frumpy little beat girl.

She takes a sip of her coffee. "Not my song," she reminds Fat Michael, even though she knows it's like trying to lose a high school nickname.

Gay Michael pulls the annex curtain aside. "I have to drive it over at lunchtime," he says, meaning the Milton.

"She won't come here?" says Fat Michael.

"What, and leave the 'two-one-oh?" Gay Michael says. "She'd melt like Margaret Hamilton." He raises a pre-emptive hand before Fat Michael can object further. "I am not risking losing this sale, Michael," he says. "It's two month's rent."

"It's just that I have that, you know, that thing," says Fat Michael.

"I'll mind the store," Bethany says. She knows that 'that thing' means a lunch date with a woman from whatever dating service he's currently using. She also knows it won't work out, they never do, but Fat Michael is a tryer and Bethany sort of loves him for it.

She's never been left alone in charge of the store because the Michaels always stagger their lunch-hours, so her offer to tend it for a couple of hours without adult supervision prompts, big surprise, a discussion. But they do their best not to make a drama out of it—which Bethany appreciates 'cause God knows it's an effort for both of them—and it boils down to her receiving several over-cautious instructions, all of which pretty much translate as *don't do anything stupid*. After she promises that she'll do her best not to, they take her up on it and Gay Michael's gone by 11:45 to beat traffic and Fat Michael's out of there by noon.

Which is how Bethany comes to be alone when the man in the Chinese Laundry initiates the Apocalypse.

Bethany's lost in her Kelly Link collection when the old-school bell tinkles on the entrance door. She looks up to see the door swinging shut behind a new customer as he walks in, holding a hardcover book in one gloved hand.

Huh, Bethany thinks. Gloves.

They're tight-fitting gray leather and, given that it's spring in California, would look even odder than they do were it not that the man's pretty over-dressed anyway. His suit is a three-piece and its vest sports a chain that dangles in a generous curve from a button and leads, Bethany presumes, to a pocket-watch that is currently, well, pocketed.

He's not in *costume* exactly, Bethany realizes—the suit is of modern cut and fit—but he's hardly inconspicuous. She flashes on the elderly Hispanic guy she and Mr. Slater had seen at the light earlier and wonders if she somehow missed the memo about this being Sharp-Dressed-Man Day in Glendale. ZZ Top start riffing in her head but the accompanying mind-video is a spontaneous mash-up with Robert Palmer and his fuck-me mascarenes and Bethany makes a note to self that she needs to start spending a little less time watching *I Love the 80s*.

"I wonder if you can help me?" the customer says, coming to the counter. Cute accent. Like the guy from *House* when he's not being the guy from *House*.

"Almost certainly not," she says. "But I'll be real nice about it."

"Ah," he says, not put out at all. Far from. "I take it, then, that you are neither Michael nor, indeed, Michael?" Now he's doing the other Hugh—Grant, not Laurie—and Bethany thinks he's laying it on a bit thick but decides to gives him the benefit of the doubt.

"Just Bethany," she says.

"Exactly who I was looking for," he says, laying the book he's carrying onto the counter. "I wanted to ask you about this."

There's no such thing as a book you never see again, Fat Michael had told her, a little booksellers' secret, shortly after she started working here. *Sooner or later, no matter how rare it is, another copy comes across the counter.* He'd been trying to make her feel better because she'd fallen in love with a UK first of Kenneth Grahame's *The Golden Age* and had been heartbroken when it left the store with somebody who could afford it. He'd been right, too; in her time with the Michaels, Bethany had seen many a mourned book wander back to their inventory, including the Grahame; one of the store's free-lance scouts had scored another copy at an estate sale just a few weeks ago.

And now here comes this customer with another book, another blast from Bethany's past, from long before she worked here, but just as she remembers it; rich green cloth boards with a stylized Nouveau orchid on the front panel, its petals cupping the blood-red letters of the title.

"You do recognize it, don't you?" the man says.

"Sure," Bethany says, because she does. "*The Memory Pool*. 1917. First and only edition."

When she looks up from the book she sees that the customer is staring at her with an expression that she finds confusing, one of well-intentioned but distant sympathy, the kind of expression you might give to a recently bereaved stranger. He touches the book's front panel lightly and briefly. "Mm," he says. "And quite rare, wouldn't you say?"

"Extremely rare," Bethany says, and immediately wants to slap her stupid mouth. *Curse me for a novice*, she thinks, a mantra of Gay Michael's whenever he's made a rare misstep in a negotiation. She's only been at the store a year, really *is* a novice still, but tipping a customer off that they've got something of real value is like entry-level dumb.

"Oh, don't worry. I'm not actually looking to sell it," he says, as if reading her dismay. "Just wanted to see if you knew it."

"Huh," says Bethany because, you know, Huh.

The customer looks at her again, cocking his head as if intrigued. He extends his gloved hand across the counter. "James Arcadia," he says, as Bethany shakes it. "I think, Just Bethany, we'd best have lunch."

"Why?" she asks, and she's smiling. Not too much, though; he's cute and all but, c'mon, he has to be forty at least. Still, she's flattered. Feels like she should conference-text the Michaels. *Not so frumpy*.

Arcadia returns the smile and she's glad that his eyes are kind because it softens the blow of his reply. "We need to discuss exactly how we're going to save the world," he says.

Well, Bethany thinks, *that was dramatic*, and, as if on cue, a woman screams from somewhere beyond the store. By the time a man's voice, equally horrified, hollers *My God, look at that!*, Bethany and Arcadia have already turned to look through the window.

On the street outside, a man is melting.

He'd presumably been walking, but he's not walking anymore. He's rooted to the sidewalk, his legs already a fused and formless mass, his flesh and his clothes running in multicolored ripples of dissolution down what used to be his body as if he was some life-size religious candle burning in fast-forward.

Other people on Brand Boulevard are screaming now, some running away, some gathering to see, one idiot on his cell-phone like he could actually fetch help, another using hers to snap a little souvenir of the atrocity. A group forms around the vanishing man, circling him but not going near, as if instinctively establishing a perimeter from which to bear witness but to keep themselves safe.

From what's left of the man's face—now liquidly elongated into a vile burlesque that puts Bethany briefly and horribly in mind of Munch's screamer—he appears to be, have been, a middle-aged white guy. *He has a life*, Bethany thinks, *he has a story, has people who love him.* But he's featureless in little more than a second. One of his arms has already disappeared into the oozing chaos of the meltdown but the other is waving grotesquely free, fingers twitching either in agony or, as Bethany wonders with a devastating stab of pity, as if he just wants someone to hold his hand in farewell as he slides helplessly from life.

When there's finally nothing about it to suggest it had ever been human, the roiling mass begins to shrink in on itself, disappearing into a vanishing center as if hungry for its own destruction, growing smaller and smaller until, at last, it shivers itself into nothingness. There's not even a stain on the sidewalk. It's taken maybe seven seconds.

"Oh my God," says Bethany.

Arcadia is keeping his eyes on the window. "Watch what happens next," he says. And when Bethany does, she decides that it's even more appalling than what came before.

Everybody walks away.

There's a blink or two from one or more of them, and one older woman in a blue pantsuit looks to her left as if she thought her peripheral vision may have just registered something, but there's no screaming, no outrage, no appeals to heaven or cries of *what-just-happened?* Everybody on the street quietly moves on about their day, neither their manner nor their expressions suggesting that anything out of the ordinary had occurred.

"What's *wrong* with them?" says Bethany. "They're all acting like it never happened."

"Don't be cross with them," Arcadia tells her. "It sort of *didn't* happen."

"But it did."

"I don't want to get too abstract about it," he says, "but it's a sort of tree falling in the forest question, isn't it? Can something actually be said to have happened if it's something nobody in the world remembers?"

"*I* remember," Bethany says.

Arcadia holds her gaze for a second or two, his face expressionless. "A-ha," he says quietly.

Bethany's still trying to think about that when he pulls his watch from his vest pocket and checks it. "Hmm," he says. "Only eleven minutes in and already a serious anomaly. That's a bit worrying."

"What?" says Bethany, horrified as much at his calmness as at the idea that this nightmare is on some kind of a schedule.

"Clock's a-ticking," he says. "Lunch will have to wait. Come on."

Bethany's surprised to see that she's following him as he moves to the door and opens it. Perhaps it's the tinkling of the bell, perhaps just a desire to remember what she was doing the last time the world made sense, but something makes her look back at the counter.

"Wait," she says. "What about your book?"

Arcadia throws it an unconcerned glance. "Do you know what a MacGuffin is, Bethany?" he says.

"Yes," she says, because she does. She watches her fair share of Turner Classic Movies and she briefly dated a guy who once had an actual name but whom she's long decided will be known to her memoirs only as The Boy Who Loved Hitchcock.

"Well, the book's a MacGuffin," Arcadia says. "It's not *irrelevant*—I mean, it never existed and yet you remember it, which is good for a gasp or two and certainly pertains to the matter at hand—but it's real function is this: To propel us headlong into a thrilling and probably life-threatening adventure. You good to go?"

He waves her through the door with a hurrying motion and they're on the street and walking south before Bethany can get her question out.

"What do you mean, 'it never existed'?" she says.

"Well, not in this particular strand of the multiverse. It's a crossover, like the unfortunate gentleman outside your shop. Do you have a car, by the way?"

"No," she says. "I mean, not here."

"Oh," he says, stopping in front of a green Mercedes. "Let's take this one, then." He opens the passenger door for her, apparently without needing a key. Bethany doesn't ask. Nor does she look too closely at how he starts it up before making an illegal U-turn and heading down Brand towards Atwater Village.

"What are we *doing*?" she asks, because she figures it's about time.

"Well, we're fixing a hole—"

"Where the rain gets in?" she says, flashing absurdly on the Beatles vinyl she'd rescued from her Dad's stuff.

"Would that it were merely rain," he says. He nods toward the sidewalk they're speeding past, and Bethany looks to see a small boy turning to green smoke while pedestrians stare open-mouthed and his screaming mother tries to grab him, her desperate fingers clawing only at his absence. By the time Bethany has swung in her seat to look out the rear window the smoke has vanished and the crowd, including the mother, has forgotten it was ever there.

Bethany's eyes are wet with pity as she turns back to Arcadia. "Tell me what's happening!" she almost shouts.

Arcadia swings the car into the right lane as they pass under the railroad bridge. "I'll try to make this as quick as I can," he says, and takes a preparatory breath. "The spaces between the worlds have been breached. Realities are bleeding through to each other. People who took one step in their own dimension took their next in another. What you've witnessed is the multiverse trying to correct itself by erasing the anomalies. Problem is it's happening in each reality and the incidents will increase exponentially until there's nothing left in any of them." He turns to look at her. "With me so far?"

Bethany unfortunately *is* with him so far, though she wishes she'd heeded those schoolyard theories that comic books weren't really for girls. "Collapse of the space-time continuum," she says in a surprisingly steady voice.

"Precisely," says Arcadia, pleased that this is going so well. "A return to a timeless shining singularity without form, thought, or feeling."

"But how?" she says. "And why?"

Arcadia has started to slow the car down now, scanning the storefronts of Atwater Village's main drag. "Because about seventeen minutes ago, something that's lived all its life as a man remembered what it really is and spoke certain words of power."

Bethany doesn't like the sound of that at all and, as Arcadia pulls up outside one of the few remaining un-gentrified stores on a strip that is mostly hipper new businesses and milk-it-quick franchises, she stays silent, feeling the sadness and fear tightening in her stomach like cancer, thinking of people vanishing from the world like a billion lights blinking out one by one.

"Is this where we're going?" she finally says, nodding at the store as they get out of the car.

"Yes," Arcadia says. "Have you seen it before?"

Bethany nods, because she has. It could have been here since 1933, she's always thought; peeling red paint on aged wood; plate-glass window whitewashed from the inside to keep its secrets; and a single hanging sign with the hand-painted phrase, *Chinese Laundry*. She doesn't think she's ever seen it open for business. "I always figured it was a front for the Tongs," she says as if she was kidding, but realizes as she says it that that actually *is* what she's always thought.

"You're such a romantic," Arcadia says, and he sounds delighted with her. He opens the door to the laundry and leads her inside.

Its interior is as weathered and as free of decoration as the outside. A hardwood floor that hasn't seen varnish for decades and utterly plain walls painted long ago in the kind of institutionally vile colors usually reserved for state hospitals in the poorest neighborhoods. Bethany is surprised, though, to smell the heavy detergent and feel the clammy humidity of what is clearly a working laundry. There's even the slow hissing, from behind the screen space-divider, of a heavy-duty steam press. The place isn't menacing, merely nondescript. The fifty year old man behind the bare wood counter would be nondescript too, were it not for the subtle phosphorescent glow of his flesh.

Arcadia makes the introductions. "Bethany Lake," he says—and Bethany registers the use of the surname she hadn't told him—"meet the entity formerly known as Jerry Harrington."

Bethany gasps a little as the man fixes his eyes on her because they are the almost solid black of a tweaker on an overdose about to kill him.

Not Chinese at all, a part of her brain wastes its time thinking, and wonders if it's entirely PC of him not to have changed the name, however generic, of the business he bought.

"What do you want?" Harrington says. His tone is hardly gracious, but at least it still sounds human, for which Bethany is grateful.

"What *do* we want?" she says to Arcadia.

"Well, *I* want him to stop destroying reality," Arcadia says. "Don't you?"

"Yes," Bethany says. "Of course."

Arcadia turns back to Harrington. "There you go," he says. "Two votes to one. Majority rules. What do you say?"

Harrington laughs, but there's little humor in it.

"What *is* he?" Bethany asks Arcadia quietly. She's turned her head away from Harrington because his face seems to be constantly coming in and out of focus in a way that she finds not just frightening but physically disturbing.

"A being from a time outside time," Arcadia says. "There's several of them around, hidden in the flesh since the Fall. Most of them don't remember themselves, but occasionally there's a problem."

The Fall? Bethany hesitates to ask, because she doesn't want to say something that sounds so ridiculous but she supposes she has to. "Are you talking about Angels?" she says. "Fallen Angels?"

"Well, you needn't be so Judeo-Christian specific about it," he says, a little sniffily. "But, yes."

"What do you want?" Harrington says again, exactly as he'd said it before. So exactly that it creeps Bethany out. Less like a person repeating themselves and more like someone just rewound the tape.

"We're here to make you reconsider," Arcadia says. "We can do it the hard way, if you want, but I'd prefer to talk you out of it."

Again, the laugh. But there's little human in it.

Arcadia moves closer to the counter, which Bethany finds almost indescribably brave. "Look, I get it," he says. "You're homesick. You want a return to the *tabula rasa*, the blank page, the white light, the glorious absence. You yearn for it like a sailor for the sea or a child for its mother. You're disgusted by all this...this..." he waves his hands, searching for the words, "...all this multiplicity, this variousness, this detail and color and noise and *stuff*."

"You talk too much," Harrington says, and Bethany, though shocked at her treachery, thinks he's got a point.

"But isn't there another way to look at it?" Arcadia says. "We're all going back to the white light eventually, so what does it matter? Couldn't we imagine looking at these people amongst whom your kind has fallen not with contempt but with delight? Isn't it possible that an angel could embrace the flesh rather than loathe it? Could choose to be humanity's protector rather than its scourge?"

"You can imagine whatever you like if it makes you feel better," Harrington says, and his voice is confident and contemptuous. "But you won't imagine it for very long. Because that's not the path I've chosen."

Arcadia smiles, like there's been some misunderstanding. "Oh, I wasn't talking about you," he says.

Bethany is wondering just who the hell he *is* talking about when the pores of her flesh erupt and the light starts to stream from her body. The rush of release almost drowns out the beating of her terrible wings and the sweet music of Harrington's scream.

Arcadia picks up the small pitted cinder-like object from the laundry counter with a pair of tweezers. It's still smoking slightly and he blows on it to cool it before dropping it into a thin test tube which he slips back into an inside pocket of his suit.

"I'll put it with the others," he says to Bethany. She wonders where the *if that's alright with you* tone has come from, like he's her Beautiful Assistant rather than vice-versa, but she nods anyway. She and he are the only people in the place and she's sort of grateful that she has no memory of the last few minutes. She feels quite tired and is glad of Arcadia's arm when he walks her to the car.

Bethany's relieved that she's back in the store before either of the Michaels. As ever, there are several out-of-shelf books lying around here and there and she decides to do a little housekeeping to assuage her guilt for playing hooky. She shelves most of them in the regular stacks, some in the high-end display cases, and one in the spaces between the worlds, though she doesn't really notice that because she's thinking about her crappy Dodge and how much the shop is going to charge her to fix it this time.

Gay Michael gets back first. Maybe Fat Michael's date is going better than expected. Bethany hopes so.

"Anything happen?" Gay Michael says.

"Not so you'd notice," Bethany tells him.

ACKNOWLEDGEMENTS

My thanks to the various anthologists who were kind enough to first publish some of these stories; Michael Brown, Dennis Etchison, Del Howison & Jeff Gelb, Stephen Jones, Paul Kane & Marie O'Regan, Angus McKenzie.

Special thanks to Glen Hirshberg, not only for his kind introduction to this book but also for being my partner in *The Rolling Darkness Revue*, in the annual chapbooks of which the remainder of the stories first appeared.

Thanks, too, to the people who helped make the original British edition of this collection possible—Les & Val Edwards, Peter Coleborn, Stephen Jones, David A Sutton, Michael Marshall Smith, and Jan Edwards—and to Robert Barr and Shadowridge Press for giving it new life this side of the Atlantic.

My wife, Dana Middleton, was the first reader of all the stories. Twenty feet to the sky, moonpal.

The book's title is a riff on a chapter name from *The Great Return* by Arthur Machen, whose wisdom and brilliance deserve a much finer tribute. *Omnia exeunt in mysterium.*

PUBLICATION HISTORY

PETER ATKINS

Peter Atkins is the author of the novels *Morningstar, Big Thunder*, and *Moontown* and the screenplays *Hellraiser II, Hellraiser III, Hellraiser IV, and Wishmaster*. His short fiction has appeared in such anthologies as *The Museum of Horrors, Dark Delicacies II, Hellbound Hearts*, and *Ghosts*, and has been selected eight times for one or more of the various "Year's Best" anthologies. The UK edition of *Rumours of the Marvellous* was a finalist for the British Fantasy Award. He is the co-founder with Glen Hirshberg of The Rolling Darkness Revue, an annual folly they commit at whatever theatre will let them. He blogs at *peteratkins.blogspot.com*

www.shadowridgepress.com